THE

EBONY

TREE

MAXINE

E.

THOMPSON

Maxine E. Thompson

Milligan Books

Published and Distributed by:
Milligan Books
1425 W. Manchester Blvd., Suite B,
Los Angeles, California 90047

First Printing, May, 1995
10 9 8 7 6 5 4 3

ISBN 1-881524-44-2

Library of Congress
Cataloging in Publication Division
Library Of Congress Catalog
Card Number preassigned : 99-093101

DEDICATIONS

In loving memory of my mother, Artie Mae Vann, (1921-1993), my maternal grandmother, Lucille Cato West, (1899-1992), and my maternal great-grandmother, Virginia Cato, (approximately 1859-1931). This book is also dedicated to the line of women who went before Virginia Cato, yet were not recorded in history. Although your passage was not recorded, you have not been forgotten, for you left your fingerprint and your quest for freedom in our bloodstream.

Maxine E. Thompson

ACKNOWLEDGEMENTS

I give the glory to Jehovah God for the love I find in wordsmithing.

I thank Horace Thompson, my husband, for his love and support.

I thank my daughter, Michelle, for her spunky spirit.

I thank my son, Maurice, for his advice, "If it is to be, it is up to me."

I acknowledge my daughter, Tamaira, my son, Aaron, and my grandchildren, Briana and Brandon.

I thank my sister, Nancy Downs, for helping me to remember.

I thank Anna Rogers, who gave me the key to her apartment, left signs over her computer for me to follow, and helped me do the first proto-copy of *The Ebony Tree*.

I thank *Ebony* Magazine for giving me $1,000, in their first writing contest in 1989. This money was used to develop my craft.

I thank Marvin Dejean, author of on-line column, *Prime Directive*, whose assistance and kindness has been invaluable.

I thank Anfra Boyd, author of book and on-line column, *You are My Sister*, for her friendship, inspiration and support.

I thank Dr. Rosie Milligan, my publisher, for being a beacon of light on my spiritual path.

About The Author

Maxine E. Thompson was born and raised in Detroit, Michigan, but has resided in Los Angeles, California since 1981. After graduating from Wayne State University in Detroit, Michigan, she worked as a Child Protective Services social worker for twenty-three years, first in Detroit, then later in Los Angeles.

Ms. Thompson attempted her first novel, *The Hidden Sword*, at the age of 16, when she was the first black student to integrate St. Francis High, an all white school, in Traverse City, Michigan in 1967. In 1989, Ms. Thompson became a recipient of an honorable mention in Ebony's first writing contest for her short story, "Valley of the Shadow." In 1994, she won an award for her short story, "The Rainbow," through the International Black Writers' Association (IBWA). In 1996, she was also a recipient of a PEN award. She received certificates of merit for outstanding achievement in Writer's Digest's Self-Publishing Contests in 1995 and 1997. She has had poems, short stories, and articles published in e-zines, national magazines and anthologies. She is the author of two novels, *The Ebony Tree* and *No Pockets in a Shroud*. She also pens an Internet column, On The Same Page for new and self-published writers found at http://www.maxinethompson.com.

Maxine E. Thompson

The Ebony Tree
(For The African American Woman)

Why does no one ever laud me—
Whose sable hands calmed troubled seas?
My roots wrenched from the earth's dark bowels,
Daughters of song perched on my leaves.
Yet society applauds the white bough of the bleached birch tree,
Is it because you do not boast the ebony-hued bark like me?
Induced to shade your hallowed ground,
Your tributaries to follow,
Under your winds my branches fold,
My trunk too often made hollow....
Pruning my putrefied branches,
Yes, for the whole world to behold,
I will reclaim lost saffron shores
Of the River Nile of my soul!

- *Maxine E. Thompson, 1989*

PROLOGUE

Prologue

1993

Just as fifty-per cent of the moon is concealed from the Earth's view, the Shepherd family used speech to hide their true thoughts and feelings from one another. The family's mantra, albeit unspoken, was, "If you don't talk about it, it didn't happen."

The first time Paige realized this, the entire family was sitting around the television, watching a video which the younger sister Morgan—whose Swahili name was now Imani—had taped on the previous year. Throughout the unreeling of the tape, Morgan—rather Imani— tried to learn some family history from their parents, Jewel and Solomon Shepherd. She might as well have tried to catch hot missiles in her bare palms.

The video rolled on for an hour before Paige realized that Jewel, their mother, hid between the bushes of her words. A laconic person by nature, Jewel seemed to have forgotten all that she didn't want to remember. And that which memory allowed to dribble through her lips was suddenly imbued in rose-colored hues. On the other hand, Solly, their father, raced a world through his mouth as he shared his misty-colored-waters version of the fifty-three year marriage.

In the history of recorded misalliances, no two

people had ever been more different. Yet, strangely, the halcyon bird of peace had flown into their lives over the years, turning the raging rivers of their marriage into a windless pond, with only a murmuring of what used to be. The irony was how their jagged edges, over the crevices of time, had melded together, leaving only a hint of the fissure.

Had Imani paid attention, she would have noticed how, throughout the unfolding of the tape, more could be divined about their mother from the way she intermittently picked lint from their father's cardigan sweater, chewed her Juicy Fruit gum, and sucked on her dentures, than from any words she spoke. Jewel shifted uncomfortably in her seat, as if too much truth might seep out between the cracks of memory.

The only contradiction their mother made to their father's monologue was, "No, Daddy. We didn't see 'Gone with the Wind' in 1939. We saw it in 1951, after we moved to Detroit."

"No, we didn't, Honey. We saw it in Tulsa, when they still had colored and white theaters," Solly refuted.

Their mother offered no argument. Like most longstanding relationships, theirs had survived life's storms by knowing when to defer to the other party. Solly had always been the talker, Jewel the doer. Jewel said nothing else on the matter. Once again, the balance was maintained in the marriage, and Solly retained his status as the spokesman, the lord of the family archives.

Yet the funny thing about it was, that although Solly did most of the talking, little of what he said even waved at the well of his unexpressed feelings. The disappointments, the bitterness, the frustration of being a young Black man, growing up in the South during the

4

1920's and 1930's.

All the closed doors and erected walls to opportunity that he had bumped his head against, while raising his family during the forties and the fifties. How he had, rather than talk about it, acted it out on the canvas of his life. And how he had survived it at all.

For their father, the truth would always lie buried somewhere amidst a mountain range, a river and a valley of his real emotions. So in a way, the video was true to form, a triptych, capturing the essence of their family — people saying one thing, thinking another, and meaning something altogether different.

But Imani persisted. First and foremost, she was a journalist. She wanted to know the five W's. Who, what, where, when, why? When they first moved to Delray, who did they have as friends? What had it been like living in Delray? A question she left unasked, but which still hung in the air like a vapor, was, "Why did you have me so late in life?"

Born in the autumn of their parents' lives, Imani had grown up in the cloistered world of older parents. She had six older brothers and sisters, most of whom were married from the time she could remember. In fact, they were so many continents removed from her in upbringing, tastes, and interests, she felt like a changeling left on the doorstep of this family. As a journalist, she had already lived in Russia and Paris, so although she was only twenty-six, she felt like she was worldly enough of a traveler to understand her family. As a child, she'd merely viewed her siblings as "old people."

But as an adult, she viewed most of them as "crazy." Even if there was an engineer, psychologist, business owners, and even a professional writer numbered among them, they were so different from her. A perpetual bubble of violence always percolated under their skins, threatening to erupt like a volcano.

How had they sprang from the same loins? Why were they so different from her? Why wouldn't her mother tell her anything about her past?

Imani wanted to know. . . .

BONDAGE

Fall, 1950

Delray, Michigan

Anger blindfolded Jewel. Stalking up Cottrow Street at twilight, Jewel refused to be dazzled by the magenta, russet and scarlet leaves preening on the elms overhead. Neither was she fazed by the crunch of the dead amber leaves under her feet. The only colors that Jewel could see and hear were the bright red and orange sparks swirling through her brain. The colors reminded her of the lightning bugs from the summer nights of her childhood in Oklahoma years ago.

But there was no time to visit a summer that lay avalanched under the snows of twenty-five years. Today, she had to deal with the demons of the present. And unlike her neighbors, she refused to sit back on her porch and simply wait for whatever life trickled out to her.

"Mama, where we going?" Cake Sandwich, her oldest son, asked, struggling to keep up with his mother's brisk steps. The little boy's short legs felt like paddle wheels on a steamboat, as he strained to pull his four-year-old brother, Joey, in a homemade scooter. Sweat zigzagged from his forehead, down into his eyes, nearly blinding him. The boy wiped his eyes with the back of his hand.

"Walk up," his mother hissed through her nose.

Cake Sandwich glanced back at his brother, Judge, who at eight, was one year his junior. Judge wasn't keeping up, he noticed, and he wasn't tied down with dead weight like Cake Sandwich was. Just thinking of the unfairness of it all, he stuck out his tongue at Judge.

"Mama's boy!" Cake Sandwich whispered to Judge. The older brother always took delight in taunting Judge, who had a perpetual stutter. Because of his stutter, Judge was often too slow on his feet to make a flippant retort.

"Shut up," Martha Grace, his younger sister, said between clenched teeth. Experience had taught her how to read her mother like a barometer. Although she was only six, Martha Grace could gauge Jewel's mood by the firm set of her mother's thin golden shoulders. She could also tell by the way Jewel's pocketbook slapped against the skirt of her calico dress that her mother was furious.

Being the middle child—the only female of five children—Martha Grace knew better than to ask any questions. Besides, it took all of her energy and concentration to push one-year-old Baby Boy, her youngest brother, in his carriage. The carriage—after servicing two babies and several dolls—was a mere skeleton of what it used to be. The leather sides were worn through and had to be padded with baby blankets. The hood was only a frame. With the wheels creaking and careening to the left, the carriage just limped along, hitting every bump and crack in the sidewalk.

At a distance, Martha Grace looked like a little boy. With a short braid on the top of her head, the rest of her hair fanned out in a woolly cap around her skull. To make matters worse, she was dressed in the same denim overalls all four of her brothers wore. But she thought like a little woman.

She wondered why her brothers were so dense. Didn't they do this every Friday that Daddy didn't show up by sundown?

"Oooh-weee! Something stinks!" Cake Sandwich wrinkled up his hose. "OoohOOohwee! Judge farted!"

Prancing from foot to foot, Cake Sandwich pointed at his brother. Cake Sandwich was so happy to report something bad on Judge—"Precious Judge"—that his face rippled with glee. He hoped that Mama would make Judge pull Joey in the wagon, now. Even though it was a scooter, the boys called their homemade contraption "a wagon."

This was the wagon that served as a newspaper carrier when the two boys delivered papers. The boys also collected empty pop bottles in this wagon. With the money they earned, they bought candy and marbles. But on Friday evenings, the wagon was a baby carrier.

Suddenly, a foul odor permeated the air. Judge—always sparse with words—pointed at a steaming pile of manure. The culprit—an old roan horse—driven by the local vegetable man, whom everyone called Hobo Joe, had halted in the middle of Cottrow Street and refused to budge.

Every Friday, Hobo Joe drove his dray, loaded with vegetables, up Cottrow Street. He was a white man in a sea of dark faces.

"Geddy up!" As the little monkey-faced man snapped the reins on the horse's haunches, his white grizzly hair stood up on his head like soldiers of centipedes. The children could see that he was perturbed.

He knew that no one would ever buy any of his wares if he left the horse standing around in its own manure. Finally, with a lurch, the vegetable wagon rattled, squeaked, and lumbered on like an arthritic, old man. Laughter started as a rumbling in Cake Sandwich's belly, then caused him to bend over, holding his stomach. He couldn't help   himself, as he rocked with giggles. This outburst of mirth somehow violated the sacred arena of silence of their little group.

The dying autumn day, tinged with blithe bird song, suddenly disappeared. The only sound the boy could hear centered in the ringing in his ears. Jewel had turned around and boxed one of the boy's ears before he knew what was happening.

"But Mama — " The stern look on Jewel's brow cut off Cake Sandwich's protests. What did he do wrong? He wondered. Mama never said anything to Judge. Jewel, not paying the child any more attention, turned away and picked up her strident march.

Cake Sandwich's mind was in a turmoil. How come every time Mama got mad at Daddy, he became Solly Junior instead of her beloved "little Cake Sandwich?" Why did Mama's lips — yes, those very lips which could smother him in buttery kisses — get so little at times like these that they almost disappeared into her head like those of the white women in the movies at the picture show? When she was humming and happy, he was her little "Cake Sandwich." Puzzled, he shook his head. Mama was a locked box, an enigma he could not quite fathom.

As for Jewel, her mind was a dervish maze of worry. Worrywart, that was her. Now take Solly, her husband. He was more like the grasshopper. Live for today. Play all summer. Don't worry about putting up anything for the winter.

Of the two, she was more like the ant. Even now, she was still canning from her garden, trying to put up for the winter.

Why just the other week, Solly's friend, John Henry Jackson, had come over in the middle of the night slobbering like crumpled milkweed.

"My wife gon' kill me. Solly, will you go over there and tell her I didn't mean to lose my check? Tell her I wasn't drunk."

As tears flowed down his cinnamon cheeks, John Henry's face, distorted with drink, grimaced into maudlin rivers. His features sagged into a clownish, upside-down smile.

If that wasn't the biggest lie Jewel had ever heard! It was a lowdown-dirty shame how that man carried on, with him and Frannie having five babies. Mph!

Drunk as a skunk, he was. Well, by God, if it took every ounce of strength in her body, Solly wasn't going to do that to her. Oh no! Not as long as her name was Jewel Mae Shepherd.

What with Baby Boy needing hard-bottom shoes, Cake Sandwich needing pants, seeing as how she couldn't hand anything down to him—Lord have mercy! Jewel had left a white trail of diapers flapping on the clothes line. Like a vision of white sea gulls, the windblown diapers flashed across the screen of her mind. She still had a dozen more loads of clothes to wash and only a handful of soap powder left. She hated using Fels Naptha soap, since it didn't lather as well, or get the clothes clean enough. Thinking of the basement where she washed, she remembered that the coal furnace, adjacent to the wash room, was still broken. Money was slim and the furnace needed a new motor. . . and winter was just a few months away. Lord have merciful Fathers!

The very thought of winter's blustery fangs propelled her feet to a desperate trot. Sweat began to run down her back, making her dress cling to her skin. Perhaps it wasn't too late!

"Hurry up, Heifer!" Jewel couldn't help the venom jarring each chord in her voice whenever she addressed Martha Grace, her only daughter, whom the neighbors had christened "Midge."

If the vein of truth could have been blasted from the flinty bedrock of bitterness, worry and inarticulateness, her love would have been revealed. Jewel didn't mean to be so short with Midge most of the time, but she was. She just couldn't seem to help herself. It seemed like whenever Jewel looked at Midge, she saw herself. A girl child. One without a future. Just like hers.

It all ended up the same way for girl children. Look at her life. At twenty-nine, Jewel's life had erected bars and jailed her in a dreary prison.

But a golden glimmer shined inside her whenever Jewel thought of her boys. Now boys—well, boys. . . .they were different. For her boys, she could dare dream. They had a chance to be somebody in life.

Midge grinned affably, as if nothing bothered her. She did all she could to dovetail Jewel's rapid footsteps. Why didn't Mama like her? she wondered. She always tried to help. Why, she could cook corn bread better than a woman! At six-and-a-half, Midge hoisted herself upon a stool by the O'Keefe stove and slid the corn bread into the oven. Daddy liked corn bread with his pinto beans.

Sometimes, in moments of empty spaces, it worried

Jewel that Midge was as pliable as rolled, kneaded dough. On the one hand, the child's eagerness to please bothered her, yet on the other, whenever Jewel saw any signs of rebellion, she rubbed them out.

Without warning, Baby Boy popped his head through the naked frame of the buggy hood, giving his glass bottle a jaunty toss.

"All gone," he announced, proud of stringing together his first sentence at fifteen months. The glass shattered and splintered all over the sidewalk.

A twig snapped inside of Jewel's already tethered psyche. Her nerves, glued together by a frazzled shoestring, were as tattered as anybody's worn-out coat, and split in half. Thoughts, emotions, and feelings scrambled around inside of her, toppling reason awry.

"Pick up that glass, Heifer!"

Her mother's raised scolding voice was the rhythm of life to Midge. She knew, in turn, that Jewel's voice could be tender, but not on Friday evenings. Midge picked up the larger shards of glass, careful not to cut her hand.

"Where should I put the glass, Mama?"

Jewel didn't answer. When Midge saw that her mother was safely ahead of her, she dropped the glass in the gutter at the curb's edge.

As they continued up the street, desultory conversation eddied and filled the air. The neighbors, seduced by the last warmth of summer, were gathered on their porches.

"Nice day today, Miss Jewel."

"Sho' was hot today. Think it'll rain?"

The neighbors knew by the tomahawk gleam in Jewel's beady eyes that this was not a day to be catty with her. Piercing the landscape of her high Indian cheekbones, the smoldering coals of her eyes flashed. From her front porch, her neighbor, Miss Lenore, sat combing her daughter Mary Kate's hair. Miss Lenore pinioned the child's head and shoulders between her knees, as she dipped a hairbrush between a glass of water, a jar of Dixie Peach, and the child's bushy cloud of hair. Nimbly braiding it into two shoulder-length, horn-shaped braids, her hands, looking like that of a weaver's, were a study in rhythm and motion. Over Mary Kate's head, Miss Lenore nodded at Jewel with understanding. Everyone knew "The Look." It was pay day.

On pay days, as they waited, all of the women seemed to be pregnant with longing. United by a common cause and bound by a veil of silence, the row of clapboard houses crouched together like cats ready to pounce on their prey. The languid streets, earlier filled with the teeming sounds of children, were suddenly hushed, subdued. The leftover, mingled smells of the evening meals' fried chicken, pinto beans, and collard greens wafted and lingered throughout the silent streets.

The subjects of this palpable yearning were generally in the employ of Chrysler, Ford, Great Lakes Steel, or Michigan Melville. These were the husbands, the breadwinners, the ones upon whom their livelihoods depended.

None of the other women had the nerve to do what Jewel did every pay day that Solly was gainfully employed. She believed in the power of prayer. However, she also believed that God helped those who helped themselves. Particularly on a husband's pay day.

Jewel and her neighbors were all children of the

South who had migrated North, looking for a better life. A life away from a blinding sea of cotton fields, sharecropping shacks, and unending, backbreaking toil. Instead, what they had found when they "come North," was the gangrene of crusted disillusionment, the cancer of splintered dreams, and the leprosy of gnarled spirits. They could all taste the absinthe of Jewel's disappointment. True, they all thought Jewel was just a little too prissy for their tastes. They didn't like the fact that she never suckled her babies or combed her daughter's hair on the front porch.

Jewel never shouted in church or "got happy," as they called it when the Holy Ghost hit you.

Whereas the other neighborhood women ran in and out of each other's homes, borrowing an egg or a cup of sugar, Jewel fed people "out of a long-handled spoon" and kept to herself. She never asked anyone for anything, and except for Solly's brother, A.J. and his wife, Cleotha, she rarely had company. This, to the others, was the height of rudeness.

Jewel's biggest sin—the predilection for which her neighbors could not forgive her—was that she never shared her thoughts, feelings, and business with anyone. It was for this reason, her neighbors took such pleasure in criticizing her behind her back.

"Mark my words. Jewel's going to come to a fall one day."

"Thinks she's better than us."

"She think she's something because she is high-yellow."

Gossip and small talk being the diastole and systole of Delray, the neighbors took even greater pleasure in trying to bring Jewel down a peg or two by reporting

Solly's comings and goings.

"Jewel, we just seen Solly over at Miss Bertie's."

"Solly down to the beer garden."

"Solly over at the juke joint."

Never mind that none of this information was summoned, but there was always a willing newsmonger. They all wanted to see a reaction. Much to their disappointment, Jewel's face remained as inscrutable as a closed casket. The closest anyone came to knowing how Jewel's personality was wired and what stirred the still waters of her character came on Friday at vespers.

Then, as they later reported to each other, the neighbors could hear "arguing-a-plenty" over Solly's pay check. But Jewel kept her mouth shut. People had to guess about her. They could confabulate and think whatever, but she never opened her mouth and confirmed anything.

Never would you catch Jewel chatting over her fence, commiserating with a friend, "Girl, Solly got drunk last night."

For what was on Jewel's mind, no one else could understand. Jewel had pictures in her head, for which she had no words yet. In these pictures, she was going to get out of Delray one day. Her children were going to be somebody. They weren't always going to be little. With that thought in mind, Jewel unconsciously threw her head back, tilting her slim neck at a haughty slant. Unknowingly, she was a flamingo in a river bed of cranes.

There was an imperceptible quality about Jewel, an air of arrogance, which made people call her "The Duchess of Delray." This proud, regal bearing—the one that her grandfather, Noble Hightower, had instilled in Jewel—branded her as an outcast in Delray. She would never quite fit in, and she really didn't care.

Yes, she had dreams. Pearly-gate dreams. That was the reason she took her children to the library. What did dreams cost? Dreams were free.

Jewel quickened her step when she reached Solvan Street. South Bend divided Delray into two worlds. Jewel's street, Cottrow, was inhabited from one end of the street to the other by the churchgoing denizens. Solvan, on the other hand, was peopled by two castes of characters.

On the west end of Solvan, the law-abiding citizens, peppered by a few storekeepers, abided in relative harmony. At the eastern end of the street, the "sporting-life" vultures rapaciously preyed on the carrion of each other's lives.

"The Block," as it was called, consisted of two city streets of pool rooms, brothels, bars, and a greasy-spoon restaurant run by a bootlegger named Skeeter and his corpulent wife, Addie Mae. The street came alive every weekend with knifings and shootings, so much so that they called it "The Chopping Block." Later, the name was shortened to "The Block."

The dregs of Delray, scorned by all the "good churchgoing people," lived a nocturnal life. Its citizens were just taking their first yawn into awakening when Jewel walked by with her children.

Generally, Jewel didn't like to pass this street after dusk. Hadn't a woman been killed over there last week? Well, tonight, she didn't care. With eyes of daggers, she dared any of these roughnecks to try to lay a hand on her or her babies.

A group of men, shooting dice at the corner of the alley, stared at her and the children in dispassionate dryness, then turned back to their game. Jewel stepped fastidiously around the neighborhood wino, Hambone, who had passed out on the sidewalk.

"Come on," Jewel ordered, ushering her little band of children ahead of her.

"Baby needs a new pair of shoes," she heard one of the men exclaim as he tossed the dice. The group of men's raucous laughter soured the air, reminding her of the fear gnawing at the corners of her mind. Jewel needed money for more than just taking care of her children. She dreamed of fish last night. All day she'd stared repeatedly at the black circle on her calendar. It stood both as a reminder and an accusation.

She was late again. No period this month. She had already started eating dirt from the back yard. She was beginning to crave Argo starch again. Just the crunch in her mouth sent rapturous thrills through her body. She knew it was crazy, but she baked the gray topsoil in an effort to sterilize it. The fear gnawing at the corner of her mind could not accept this predicament in which once again, her body had betrayed her dreams.

Jewel finally reached Scotty's Beer Garden. The local tavern couldn't have been more strategically located across from Solly's job at Michigan Melville than if Scotty had planted it there. It was like the nectar of a flower to a bee. Solly was drawn to go there, claiming he needed "peace and quiet" from Jewel and the kids, but Jewel knew Solly's true reason.

"Wait here." Jewel wasn't speaking to anyone in particular, as she left the little band of children on the corner facing both the west side of the bar and the setting sun. Jewel glanced back at her children.

Daniel, whom they had nicknamed Baby Boy, had

fallen asleep in his carriage. Joey, sucking on the edge of his tee shirt, sat contentedly in the scooter. The big kids called Joey "Liver Lips" and "Juice Mouth" when they thought that Jewel wasn't listening. They nicknamed him this, because he always had a steady stream of saliva trickling down his chin onto his undershirts. Still, Jewel thought that he had been her prettiest baby out of the bunch. Brown taffy skin and big black curls. Thinking of hair, Jewel looked over at Midge — really studied her — for the first time that day. Without a ribbon in her short beady hair, her daughter couldn't be distinguished from her brothers. The whole group was a pitiful "throwed-away looking bunch," Jewel admitted to herself. Even though she knew they looked clean enough, despair punched her in the stomach. What was she going to do?

The marquee lights outside Scotty's Beer Garden flashed on and off like a red lighthouse tower, casting blood-tinted shadows into the dusk. Jewel recognized the advertised blues singer—Sadie Mae Hawkins—as the same woman who doubled as the cocktail waitress. The windows, stained from tar and nicotine, reminded Jewel of "the den of iniquity" that the pastor railed against on Sundays, whenever she could make it to church. A bluesy dirge, belting out of the juke box, crept on wailing feet from under the door sill. Fried fish grease and stale, unfermented beer wafted on the air. Jewel hesitated at the door. Timid in that "good women" never frequented this type of place, she craned her neck and peered through the window, shading her eyes to adjust them to the dimness inside of the barroom.

Emboldened by what she saw, Jewel threw the door open.

"Solomon Shepherd! If you don't get over here, you better! You know good and well I was waiting on you." Standing arms akimbo on her gaunt hips, Jewel's voice held the quiet undertow of dangerous flood waters. Approximately ten feet from her, eyes squinted in a glassy, drunken stupor, Solly half-leaned, half-stood over a round table covered with a checkered oilcloth. Jewel's eyes traveled down to his large brown hands encircling a foamy mug of beer. His dark brown features—the color of polished onyx—once so handsome to her—ran together like a broken egg. His neon-red eyes blazed with the shock of recognition when he saw Jewel.

Nothing but the Devil. At that moment, Jewel hated him more than anyone she'd ever known. Their personalities were so different, it was as though she was staring at him from a separate shore. How had she ever married this stranger?

In a sudden wave, the stench of cigarette smoke, cheap perfume, and rotgut whiskey crashed all over Jewel, making her want to throw up. She swallowed back the bile scorching the roof of her throat. In that instant, she realized it was hopeless. Jewel wanted to cry, but her eyeballs felt as dry as parched maple leaves seared by an Indian summer sun.

What was the use? Her life reminded her of the mulberry tree in her backyard. Although they were not particularly edible, the mulberries grew by the bushels each summer. Whenever they fell, staining the sidewalk a purplish-blood color, Jewel would feverishly sweep them up. No sooner than she'd clear them away, a fresh new crop would fall on the ground, and she'd have to start all over again.

It was the same thing with the grass seeds she planted every year. The children turned around and trampled down all but a few blades, leaving the yard with a slate gray, barren look. Even worse, the mulberry tree killed what was left of the grass.

Sometimes, in moments of desperation, Jewel thought about cutting down the mulberry tree, but she never did. One reason was that she liked to write to her relatives in Vernon and Tulsa, Oklahoma, telling them about the beautiful fruit tree she had in her back yard. Of course, she never mentioned that it was a useless, old mulberry tree. She also failed to mention that her "brick home" was built from an artificial brick material which covered the clapboard. All she knew was that it was hers. She — well, she and Solly — were buying it for seventy-five dollars a month. She'd always vowed this one thing; she wasn't going to spend her life renting like those other shiftless, improvident neighbors of hers. No, not Jewel.

"Mama, hurry up!" Cake Sandwich clamored from around the corner, interrupting her reverie. "It's getting dark out here."

"Solomon Shepherd! If I have to cross this threshold, Lord knows, your drunk ass will be sorry."

Jewel's pupils, scintillating in her brown eyes like lightning, belied the low tone of her voice. Fortunately, Solly, who had learned to identify this tone of voice as the one which preceded the dangerous floodgates in Jewel, was sober enough to try to placate her.

"Jewel. . . .Honey. . . .I just stopped for a beer." Solly's words, in an effort not to sound drunk, tripped over each other.

Jewel stared at his crooked, drunk smile — the one which used to melt her like molasses oozing out of a hot, split biscuit.

"Don't let me say it again, Solly."

With difficulty, Solly stumbled to his feet and weaved over to the door. His steps left a zigzag line through the sawdust sprinkled on the barroom's floor.

For the first time, Jewel noticed the other men and women sitting around the circular tables in the bar. She could tell from their quiet stares that she had interrupted a rendezvous. Jewel's eyes zeroed in on one woman in particular. Eldoretha Gray. In her heart, Jewel knew that this floozy was Solly's outside woman. Unfortunately, that was just a luxury she couldn't afford to worry about at that moment.

That was one lesson that she'd learned from Mama Lovey, her grandmother, who had raised her. How to look the other way. Besides, she had to get that check. She had her babies to feed.

Mama Lovey had borne eighteen children for Grandpa Hightower, whom Jewel had called "Papa." Yet to his dying day, Papa had kept "a bad woman." The adulteress in question was named "Miss Trudy."

When Jewel was growing up, "Miss Trudy" was a hissing sound which whispered in the corners of the house. Miss Trudy lived down the road from them in Vernon, Oklahoma. Every Sunday, after attending church with his family, Papa ate dinner, lit up his corncob pipe, then hitched up his pinto horse whom he called "Mule." Just as the animal's name implied, Mule was as fractious and recalcitrant as they came.

Each day at noon, Mule would stop pulling the plow, bolt from the fields, and trot until he reached the water trough. No amount of beating could break this habit. Finally, everyone accepted the fact that Mule quit work at high noon. Actually, the two mules, Sam and Blade, had to do most of the work. But Papa and Mule were a team. They went everywhere together, including to Miss Trudy's.

It was common knowledge among the eighteen offspring who were still living at home and the grandchildren that whenever Papa hitched up Mule on Sunday, he was going to see "Miss Trudy." Generally, after he left, Mama Lovey would spit in the dust kicked up by Papa's retreating carriage, then snort out, "Miss

Trudy!" As long as she lived, Jewel would never forget the jaundiced look and spiteful hiss which issued from Mama Lovey's nostrils. Yet, whenever Papa would come home, Mama Lovey would never utter a word of reproach to him. That was how Jewel learned to turn a blind eye to what she didn't want to see.

"Get your ass home," Jewel said one last time. She impaled Solly with her embittered glare. Before Jewel could take a step forward, Solomon started for the door.

"I was coming home. You didn't have to come down here, embarrassing me. I'm getting tired of this now."

Solly tried to regain some of his lost dignity in front of his consort by donning a cloak of indifference.

Jewel simply ignored Solly. Flanked by her man and her children, with back ramrod stiff for the sake of wagging tongues, Jewel marched her family home. It was a faintly luminous night. Cottrow Street only had two lampposts situated at each end of the street. The sidewalks were bathed in glimmers from a constellation of stars which looked as if they were petals of silver sprinkled on the earth.

Once the family made it inside their house, the children instinctively went into the kitchen. Being the nucleus of their home life, the kitchen had a life of its own. Not only was it the heart of the home, it was like a bicycle spoke in relation to the five rooms sprawling around it. Midge took Baby Boy out of his carriage and began to cuddle him. She and her brothers sat on their backless chairs, looking alert as roaches waiting for the lights to go out.

When she saw her parents go into their bedroom, Midge held her breath. Their bedroom was situated at the front of the first floor of their two-story house. The upstairs, with the same corresponding rooms, could only be reached from the back porch. Ever since Midge could remember living in this house, no one had ever lived upstairs. Although she was only a little girl, Midge knew trouble when she smelled it.

It walked in the form of the two people whom she loved the most in her young life. She waited, holding her breath, with the dull patience of an obdurate cow. Midge was oblivious to the war the radio said was brewing outside of 539 Cottrow Street over in some strange land called Korea. Her only concern was for the one brewing inside the four walls next to the kitchen door — the war which concerned her well-being.

The kitchen was the room that Midge loved the most. This was the room where they all sat down to eat meals together on chairs which, more often than not, had the backs missing. This was where Jewel usually bathed her babies in the sink until they were two years old. And this was where sweat trickled down the window panes, making Midge think the house had eyes that cried whenever a pot of beans or soup steamed up the kitchen on a wintry day. The kitchen also had a certain music to it. The sink gurgled. Leaky faucets dripped. Mice squealed, as they ran back and forth under the counters.

Today, though, the kitchen felt charged with danger, quivering in that soundless way the backyard did before a rain storm fell. That evening, this room offered no solace to the child. Midge listened for the familiar furious murmur which usually would later rise into thunder. Instead, all she heard at first was a gentle susurrus movement of the trees. Then, slowly, the wind began to rise, leaping into a war cry, rushing under the door, rustling the tree leaves against the windows like amber and golden pompoms.

In Midge's parents' bedroom, the first thing Jewel did was reach into Solly's pocket. Right away, she discovered that he was twenty dollars short of what his take-home pay should have been. A gasket blew out in the engine of Jewel's brain. She forgot who or where she was. She could still taste her frustration when, as a newlywed, Solly had spent his entire thirty-dollar check, leaving her with fifty-cents. She could still see the dead-eyed rat she'd killed with a broom earlier that morning. She'd slammed that varmint into the next world when she woke up and found it on top of Midge's quilt, its poisonous fangs posed to bite her sleeping child.

In an instant, a parade of cough syrup, shoes, and even more—a week's worth of groceries flashed on her eyeballs, just as surely as a drowning man is said to see his life flash before his eyes just before death. Simply digesting the thought of the missing twenty dollar bill, Jewel entered into a savage region in her mind—a region where speech ended and survival of the fittest reigned. All of a sudden, the bedroom, with the closet Solly had built against the north wall, felt as much prison as it did home. Now Jewel knew how trapped the rat she'd cornered and killed earlier that day must have felt. Solly was her jailer. His maleness was both lock and key. But Jewel wanted to lash out—to fight back. Yes, she wanted to draw Solly's blood! The serpents of hate found their way into the claws of her fingernails.

A slash of lightning zigzagged through the black

cloud of Jewel's anger, striking Solly in its path. With strength she, herself, didn't know she possessed, Jewel picked up a high heel and clunked Solly on top of his head. The melee was on.

"Lord, as if I don't have enough to worry with," Jewel cried over and over, swinging the shoe wildly.

Solly blocked the steady stream of blows at first. "I work my fingers to the bone around here, and you out messing up what little money we do have."

"Hey cut it out, now, Jewel. Now, Jewel, I'm not playing with you," Solly protested, sobering up a bit.

"I'll kill you, hear," Jewel hissed with all the venom she could gather in the vortex of her anger. "I tell you, I'll kill you before I see you do me like John Henry did Frannie. I'll kill you first."

Now Solly wasn't a violent man or a wifebeater. Generally, he was a happy-go-lucky drunk. But he was a man. And he knew that once Jewel got started, she was a wildcat. A regular lynx, she was.

Taking the course of least resistance, he sobered up even more and pinned Jewel down on the bed, in an attempt to stop her flailing arms and the deadly high heel.

"Oh, hold me down, will you?" Jewel spit out. "Now I'm really going to kill your drunk ass." Jewel continued to tussle, kick, squirm, bite, and scratch at Solly's large hands. Still, his hands remained a vice around her wrist. On a street where women wore the mantle of knife marks rendered by the hands of their husbands, Solly was singular in that he did not fight Jewel. Part of his reasoning was that he was proud of her good looks and didn't want to have her scarred up, walking on his arm. But the main reason was that he knew that Jewel wouldn't allow it. She was as mean as a starved alligator when she got riled up.

"I told you to stop this mess, Jewel. What's wrong with you?" Somehow, Jewel wrestled an arm loose and reached for the ashtray sitting on the bureau next to their bed. She felt her pin cushion slip beyond her reach. She heard her cardboard box filled with costume jewelry crash to the floor. Finally, Jewel's fingers found what they were searching for. She meant to club Solly on the head with the ash tray.

Instead, in the effort it took to curve the ashtray toward Solly's head, it went sailing out of her hand. At that very moment, Martha Grace had peeked around the bedroom door. When the ash tray hit her in the middle of her forehead, a geyser of blood gushed out of the child's head. For a moment, the child and the parents were frozen in space, a freeze frame. Midge's only thought was how strange her parents looked, entangled arms and legs resembling the octopus she'd seen in a book. At last, Jewel found her voice. "Now look what you did, Nigger! Made me kill my baby."

On the wall over the bed, the banner proclaiming "God Bless Our Home," shook like a leaf tossed and blown in a feckless wind. The couple disengaged themselves from one another and rushed to their daughter's side. Pandemonium ended abruptly with a trip to the hospital for stitches in Midge's forehead. Outside the brown artificial brick house on Cottrow, the autumn wind whistled and wailed through the arms of the mulberry tree like a bereft mother. More than the pain of stitches, more than the windy walk to the hospital on Jefferson Street, Midge always remembered the white towel stained like a red starfish with her blood. Jewel kept the towel plastered to Midge's forehead.

Occasionally, Jewel would lift the towel up, checking the flow of blood. She said the same thing over and over to Midge.

"Don't tell them what happened, you hear? You remember when they ask you what happened, you just tell them you fell."

Jewel needed to see Miss Mamie desperately. She was in a fix again. Oh, she could just hear and picture the disgust in her in-laws' eyes and voices.

"Jewel keep having babies."

"Mmm-mmm-mmm."

"Maybe Solly wouldn't drink so much if she didn't stay barefoot and pregnant all the time." She could just hear his sister, Gertrude.

"It's a doggone shame with Solly having two years of college at Mountain View and all. She's just taking him down."

"They can hardly afford to feed the ones they have. Must be on welfare, with Solly laid off all the time."

It really didn't matter what anyone else said. If Jewel wanted any more babies, she wouldn't have minded. But she had reached her limits. How young and naive she'd been, Jewel thought to herself, that late November morning in 1950. Now, she finally understood why her mother, Luralee, had always said, "Don't have a houseful of babies." At last Jewel knew what older people meant by the expression, "If I only knew then what I know now—."

Here she was, only twenty-nine with five babies, and if she couldn't help it, another one on the way. As a girl, she used to innocently claim that she was going to have eighteen babies like Mama Lovey.

Jewel had already lost several children through miscarriage. She had pyorrhea and was in such bad need of dental work that she seldom smiled anymore. But vanity aside, all she could think of was how they could hardly afford to feed the ones they had, let alone another mouth. If she had another baby, how would she be able to make it? True enough, Mama Lovey had raised all those children but in actuality, there had been two sets of children. The older ones were able to help provide for the younger half of the family, later even paying for the latter's educations. All eighteen children had been able to pull a plow by the time they were old enough to see the horse's behind, so living on a farm made food sufficient, if not plentiful.

But here Jewel was, living in a strange city, with hardly any relatives she could turn to for help. All of her children were under ten years of age. She had a little garden, but it hardly provided all the sustenance her children needed. From the time Jewel, with her four children in tow, climbed off the train from Richmond, California, she'd hated Detroit. She particularly hated Delray, where she'd elected to move since the property was cheap enough to be able to buy a home. No amount of soap and water could clean the dust, which settled like a charcoal mist over the little river community. Delray, an enclave in the southeast quadrant of Detroit, was hemmed in on one edge by the brackish green waters of the Detroit River and straddled on the other by railroad tracks.

Any delineation as to the "wrong side of the tracks" was all purely psychological. It was all "the wrong side of the tracks," as far as Jewel was concerned. The Detroit side of the river was bordered by a phalanx of steel mills and petrochemical plants which belched out fire and smoke, day and night. The city's air reeked of rubber and sulfur, issuing out of the UniRoyal Rubber Tire Plant, which stood guard like a sentinel soldier at the mouth of the bridge by Belle Isle Park. Often, the lurid sky painted the night a brilliant, fiery orange.

Every time Jewel hung out the wash in her backyard, grimy soot settled on the clean clothes like a fine, black drizzle. A hopeless layer of dust clung to everything, including her furniture, her floors, her walls, even her children. Even so, Jewel, like a persistent female Sisyphus, continued to push the boulder of drudgery back up the hill to have the gods roll it back down. She bathed her children every day. She attacked grime and its sister, mold, with the regularity and relentlessness of the sun. But nothing ever looked any better.

Across the river — "narrow straits" — as the French who had first settled there named it — the border of Canada loomed like a mirage of flotsam. Whenever Jewel went to River Side Park in Ecorse or to Belle Isle, she thought of Papa Hightower's story of how a group of slaves had run off from their plantation when he was a child. He had always heard it whispered that they all followed the North Star via the Underground Railroad until they made it to the Ohio River. From there, the slaves had entered Canada through the Detroit River. Jewel wondered what had become of them. Had they changed their identities?

Jewel ached to travel; she just wanted to get on a barge to see where the rivers ended. The River Rouge, she knew, was a small tributary off of the Detroit River. The Detroit River fed into Lake St. Claire and Lake Erie. But to her, the lovely park, Belle Isle, with all of its streams and beaches, had to be an estuary cut off from the sea.

Jewel loved the water so; it made her feel like she was holding a little drop of heaven in her hands. She had hopes that the tides of life would roll in, washing her into a better existence.

Travel and the call of freedom were chimeras never far from her heart. Just on hearing the clackety-clack, shilackety-lack of the trains bolting down the railroad tracks made her want to break free and run. But an invisible hand always held her back. She never forgot how abandoned she'd felt as a child. Like a mountain climber looking back down a rocky precipice, Jewel realized she had reached a new plateau in her life. Now, she finally understood why Luralee would get so upset each time she found out Jewel was pregnant. Her mother had understood better than, and before Jewel did, that each baby tied her hands and feet more.

Now Jewel could not see the cartoon strip in the newspaper with the damsel tied to the railroad tracks without seeing herself. She knew that Solly was the train barreling down the tracks of her life. Her children were the ropes. They said it was dangerous, what she was about to do. She'd even had a girlfriend named Ava who died in Oklahoma last year trying to have one. What if she died? Who would take care of her other children? Oh, she couldn't worry about that now. She was as desperate as a blind animal caught in a lair.

"Midge, watch the kids for me while I run out for a little while," Jewel said, grabbing her scarf and shawl. When she heard a small voice say, "It's going to be all right," Jewel started. Jewel looked back at Midge. Had the child said what she thought she'd heard her say? It was as if Midge could read her mind. Jewel shook her head, as she left out of the back door. That's what

bothered her about that kid. She seemed so old, like she'd
been here before. Jewel didn't realize that often, when
she was working things out in her head as to how they
were going to make it through each day, she would be
talking out loud to Midge.

She was only twenty-two years older than Midge.
How was she to know it was too heavy for a little girl to
handle all of this unburdening? She was often so
overwhelmed, she couldn't think straight. Had she had
close girlfriends, she could have confided in them. But
Jewel was very private. Right now, all Jewel was
worried about was how to get out of her predicament.
The one thing which softened some of the mundaneness
of her life was also the very thing which caused a thorn
in her side. Or rather her belly. Jewel had been
pregnant so much in the past ten years, she had become
dull inside the basin of her mind.

As she headed south towards what was called the
Low End of Delray, Jewel's heart was heavy. Whenever
anyone visited the Low End, they always said, "I'm
going to the Low End." Yet no one ever called the end
of Delray where Jewel lived "The High End." On the Low
End of Delray, a perpetual stench hung in the air like a
gust of roach spray. The offensive odor escaped from a
factory where they said they made glue from the
carcasses and offal of stray dogs. Just the smell alone
made Jewel want to vomit. The sky formed buttermilk
clouds, causing everything to be touched with a hazy
finger. The overcast day matched the gloom inside of
Jewel's soul. What could she bequeath to any of her
children—especially her daughter—besides the same
legacy of oppression, poverty, and pain? When Baby Boy
was a few months old, Doctor Baker had given her a shot.

Brought her right down, too. This time, the shot hadn't worked. Well, she'd just have to try to do something about it. Or die trying.

"And please, Lord, don't let me die," she prayed fervently, "but I've got to do what I've got to do."

Walking through the Low End, Jewel passed the section of Delray called Hunky Town because it was populated by Armenians, Hungarians, and Gypsies. She was afraid of the Gypsies with their swarthy, dirty children. Mrs. Slovik, her next-door neighbor, was Hungarian, and the two women got along just fine. Unlike her other neighbors, they both respected each other's right to privacy.

As there were only two main arteries into Delray — Jefferson and Fort Street — Jewel felt isolated, cut off from the rest of the world. The pealing of the sonorous Baptist church bell tolled in the distance and added a sense of urgency to her mission. Her feet began to fly. Last week Solly had gotten a layoff notice from his job at Michigan Melville. They probably would have to get back on welfare now. She was haunted by the thought of the Welfare Lady's eyes, squinted into caverns of disgust.

"Another mouth to feed and your husband's laid off? When will you people ever learn?" Just the thought of all the poking and prying that the Welfare Lady did made Jewel cringe. She'd never forget the time the Welfare Lady had gone so far as to call her and say, "Do you know your husband has been spending the night over at Eldoretha Gray's house?"

It was enough to make you crazy. No wonder Amanda Green was as crazy as a Betsy bug. It was one thing to have to deal with your children and your menfolk. But to have the whiteman poking in all of your business. It was just too much.

"Lord, have mercy. Don't let me go crazy," Jewel prayed. Just the thought of Amanda Green in the mental hospital sent her stomach flip-flopping like a trout on the floor of a boat. Amanda Green was a neighbor of hers. She had four children whom she'd left behind. Only she wasn't dead. Now, the oldest girl, Syreeta, had to act as a surrogate mother to her sisters and brothers while the father worked. If Jewel would allow it, Solly would have her in the nuthouse, too. If she would allow it, Solly would have her hanging her head, but she wasn't. No sirree. Kept her head high as a beanstalk.

As Jewel drew near the house set twenty feet off the sidewalk, she hesitated. Drawn venetian blinds with a tired yellow hue gave the dilapidated house a vacant look. Jewel felt a slight trembling inside of her, but she took it to be her nerves. She watched the day darken and could have sworn she was walking through a cemetery at midnight. Although everyone whispered behind her back, calling Miss Mamie "The Butcher," the number of notes which had passed surreptitiously between hands, but which directed one's path to this dark house, could not be counted over the years. Miss Mamie was rumored to be related to the Seven Sisters in New Orleans. She was also said to be a root woman, conjurer, number lady, and abortionist. The latter two claims were the most established. Not only did Miss Mamie pay promptly when one hit the number, she also sent away many relieved customers who left her door in a much lighter condition than when they first arrived. Miss Mamie led Jewel back into the kitchen, a dim dank room, reeking of camphor and sulfur. A white enamel table, with folded-down sides, stood in the middle of the room.

"Climb up." As she examined Jewel, Miss Mamie's face froze into a waxen mold. Her eyebrows, slanted in consternation, looked like furry black caterpillars. Yet her eyelids were shutters over her protruding eyeballs. "Pull your dress down," Miss Mamie finally said. Jewel pulled her dress down, wondering what the next step would be.

"Why'd you wait so late?"

"What?" Jewel thought she'd heard wrong. What was Miss Mamie talking about? Was it too late to do it today? It wasn't sundown yet.

"What?"

"You're too far gone."

"What do you mean? I only missed two months."

"Well, looking at your life line on your stomach, I'd say you're about four months along."

"I can't be."

"It happens like that sometimes. You have a period when you're actually pregnant. . . .Did you take the nutmeg ball or the quinine?"

"Yes, I did."

"It didn't bring you down?"

Jewel's stomach plummeted through her legs to the floor. The room began to swirl.

"I wouldn't be here if it had."

"Well, I've never lost a patient, and I don't intend to start now."

"I'll be all right. Please - Miss Mamie. I can't wait another day."

"Well, I don't see why you waited so long in the first place." Out of the glazed windows of Jewel's eyes, Miss Mamie's silhouette wavered, flickered, and receded.

39

At first, a moan, similar to that of a wounded animal, escaped from what sounded like a voice in Jewel's bowels. Then, the strange noise worked its way up to her throat. The sandbags holding back the dam of tears behind Jewel's eyeballs burst open.

"You've got to help me," she balled in protest, like a lusty baby as it was being thrust into the world. "I was breast-feeding, and I thought I couldn't get pregnant again."

Miss Mamie's voice softened. "What's the matter, Honey? It's not for your husband?"

"No, that's not it."

"Well, then don't worry about it. This baby may end up being somebody. In the spring, or early summer, I'd say, you're going to have a little papoose."

"But is there anything I can take?"

"You done took enough stuff to kill yourself and a baby. I think this baby was just meant to be. Like I say, if the cotton root mixed with tansy didn't work or the nutmeg and quinine, you just might as well be ready to welcome your new visitor."

Jewel thought of the bitter tea which had made her vomit until she couldn't retch out anything more than a white foam. All for nothing. Thoughts began to scurry around in Jewel's head. Baby Boy was not even out of diapers yet, and another one halfway here. At one time, she'd enjoyed babies, but now that she'd had a baby in diapers for the past nine years, she felt like her head would crack open. Endless visions of soiled diapers, clabbered milk bottles, and overflowing toilets (where the kids had accidentally dropped soiled diapers) made her head feel as if it had helium in it. One day, it would surely rise up off her shoulders like a balloon let loose by one of her children and float all over the city. How come she had to be such a breeder? Her mother, Luralee, had only had two children. Even in her mother's second marriage, Jewel was unaware of any pregnancies. Saying "Water and oil can't mix," Luralee swore by Vaseline as a contraceptive. Well, in that case, Jewel's last two babies had been "Vaseline babies."

Two of her mother's sisters, Mercy D and Sunday, had each been married over twenty years and never had given birth to a baby. Luralee always told Jewel that her younger sisters were as barren as mules because Mama Lovey and Papa had borne them so late in life.

"They came from old seed," Luralee would say. Jewel's mind returned to her problem. She could just hear her neighbors, who were known for their outspokenness.

"I saw you down at the welfare office, Jewel. Too good to speak, but you on welfare just like the rest of us."

Low-life riffraff. Jewel couldn't help it. She would never be like those women. She hated being on public assistance, which primarily consisted of food commodities. Standing in line all day had made her lose a baby about six months earlier. She recalled the miscarriage she'd had earlier that year. She'd bled enough blood to fill the Red Sea. Jewel had been so weak, she'd seen death's furry shadows hovering around the corner of her eyes. But the needs of her children had superseded the pale horse.

"Mama, we hungry."

"Mama. When you gon' get up?"

"Mama, Baby Boy's diaper done went down the toilet and it's running all over the bathroom."

Jewel needed an extra set of hands on her time and energy.

"Mama, can I have a glass of milk?"

"Mama, tie my shoe." And the one she saved for when all hell broke loose—"Lord Have Merciful Fathers"—worse yet—"Mama, can my friend come over for dinner?"

A moist blanket of gray mist fogged up the streets, as Jewel stumbled home in a blind blaze of despair. Her face was clammy with the sweat of regret. What could she do? How would she make it?

Jewel felt as ancient as time. Here she was, only twenty-nine years old. Solly was too much of a goodtimer, himself, to make having five—no six—babies an easy lot. What a fool she'd been to have wanted a large family! Well, never again! If she got through this fix—she didn't know how—she would stop having babies. Sometimes, Jewel just wanted to sleep, unmolested by someone's nagging cough.

She just wanted to get through an entire night without rubbing a menthol salve on one of her children's heaving chests, or cleaning up slimy vomit which looked like raw eggs. In order to break fevers, Jewel had discovered that if she took the heated iron and glided it over the top of the blanket, whoever the patient was would usually sweat out his cold and get well. Jewel never slept a complete night even when the children were well. She could never forget that the family had no health insurance. Because of this, her knees were darker than the rest of her body, since she stayed down on them so much. Even when her children were well, Jewel could always hear the specter of their sick whines behind the screen of her mind.

"Mama, I threw up."

"Mama, I got a sore throat. Look down my throat. Daddy don't know how to do it. I want you, Mama."

"Mama, I got a fever. Feel my head. I'm burning up."

Jewel never knew exactly how she made it home. She didn't come to herself until she stood in her garden. A few straggly sunflowers, which had survived late fall, weaved and bobbed their saffron heads at her. Jewel dropped down to her knees and languidly ran her hand over the gray topsoil. She pulled some up to her tongue. She just couldn't take another step. She glanced absently over at her bare rose bush, which, without the swaddling of its pink, red, and yellow skirts, looked as ravished as she felt. She had planted the rose bush the first spring they had moved to Delray. Every year, the children trampled it, picked off of it, and in general, abused it. But every year, in the spring, it returned like a faithful lover.

Absently, Jewel looked up at the sky, just as a light feathery snow began to fall. Filaments of pink light streaked the evening sky. Jewel knew that she was at the nadir of her life. There was no lower ebb that she could sink to. But she was going to have to put up with this situation until she could do better. If she would have to have this baby, somehow, she'd make it. Jewel knew she'd just have to swallow her pride and go on down to the welfare office the next day, since Solly had not worked long enough to draw an unemployment check. The mortgage was due, and she needed coal for the furnace. Old man winter was breathing down their necks, easing up under every crack in the house, and climbing under the covers with them at night.

In the spring, she'd have her garden again. That would help. She always went to the Farmer's Market and bought bruised pears, apples, or apricots by the bushels. That which they couldn't eat, she made Mason jars of jelly or jam out of. She also bought dented canned goods from the Salvage up on Jefferson. From the harvest of her garden, she usually had plenty of canned vegetables laid up for the winter.

Suddenly, an idea, as fructose as a warm syrup spreading over the waffles of her brain, invaded her mind. The upstairs of her house was empty. She could take in boarders. Why hadn't she thought of that before? The redolent scent of sarsaparilla from an old vine in her garden made her think of Mama Lovey, and the last winter of her life as she lay dying. Mama Lovey's sickroom smelled of sarsaparilla. Although Mama Lovey still loved her tea with sarsaparilla in it, she had been too weak and too sick to even hold the amber liquid down. Jewel had been with her grandmother when she drew her last breath, but sometimes, she could swear that Lovey had never died, she sensed her presence so. Jewel often dreamed of Lovey whenever she was troubled. Somehow, Lovey was a fly buzzing around in Jewel's head. Remembering Mama Lovey's last words, she said to herself, "This too will pass."

"**B**ecause I was the Master's half-breed, that's why I sit where I sit today."

Holding a glass of iced tea, as she reflected on her life, Mama Lovey would often make this remark. Jewel could still see her grandmother, sitting on the front verandah, facing the road, just as if it happened yesterday. Maybe it was the shades of pessimism in her voice or something about the way the light refracted on the ice cubes, but Jewel could still feel goose bumps rise up on her arms. Mama Lovey, Jewel's maternal grandmother, had been born a slave. She was five years old when "Jubilee come."

Mama Lovey always said she could remember the last of the Union soldiers marching out of Louisiana. She had been raised on the Hightower Plantation near what was now called Opelousa. As a child, Jewel loved to hear Mama Lovey tell stories about when she was a little girl during slavery. Although Mama Lovey said slavery was bad, it sounded like fun to Jewel. Her grandmother would vividly describe the dancing and singing that the slaves did when they found out that they were free. Some ran off, fighting with the last of the Union soldiers. But most of them stayed on, where they had family, roots, kinfolk.

As for Lovey, though, Emancipation had been a mixed blessing in her memory. Whereas most people would remember where they were working, walking or standing, Lovey would only think of peppermint candy and her distaste for it. Freedom had made Lovey cry. It had also marked the end of her childhood. For this was the day her mother, Oriole, informed her that the man, Fred Hightower, whom the child had thought was merely her master, was also her father.

"But, little rainbow child, you are never to tell anyone," Oriole told Lovey. Because of this new knowledge, and the way she found out, for the girl and the woman she was to become, "Freedom" would always hold the bitter aftertaste of wormwood. Up until this point, Lovey had accepted the straightness of her hair as normal. She thought that she was just like all the other slaves—except that her hair was a little straighter. Her mother, Oriole, who could not be sure of her own parentage, since she had been sold away as a young child out of Alabama, was possibly part Cherokee. Although Oriole's waist-length hair was always wrapped, it was bulrush-black and silky-straight.

As a child, Lovey never questioned why Master sometimes gave her and her brother, Caleb, peppermint candy. Candy was a rare treat for the children of slaves, but Lovey thought that it was customary for the Master to give "the little pickaninnies" sweets. Lovey had often hoarded her candy so that she could savor it longer than her brother, Caleb, who gobbled his candy down right away. But once she found out that Master Fred was her father, she hated the sight of peppermint for the rest of her life.

It seemed as if that piece of peppermint represented the evil fruit from the tree of knowledge. For it was after she ate from this bitter fruit, that Lovey's feet were set upon a hard path. From that day forth, Lovey had but one desire in her life, and that was to never be like her mother. Her mother, Oriole, had always been set apart from the other members of the slave community. Lovey had always sensed that Oriole did not quite fit in with the collective group. And if her mother, her only claim to blood kin and family she had in this world, didn't fit in, then where did she belong?

From the time Lovey could remember, Oriole had always lived alone. She was alone at prayer meetings. She never had a man in her cabin at night. Or at least that was what the child had thought. After Lovey learned about her blood tie to the Master, she began to understand who the shadowy, nocturnal visitor in their cabin was. When her mother thought that she and Caleb were asleep, the Master often slipped into the cabin. Although it was a tacit, unspoken agreement, it was common knowledge among the slaves that Oriole was the Master's woman, therefore, she was forbidden fruit to the Black bucks on the plantation. The Master's wife was a sickly woman named Sarah, who seldom, if ever, came out of the big house. Once she had seen Lovey playing with the other slave children, and it seemed as if the very sight of the child made her take to her bed again. In fact, the sight of the child was such an affront to "decent white womanhood," that Sarah remained in bed for the rest of her natural life.

As a child, Lovey used to watch the other slave couples come in from the fields, arm in arm, sometimes singing. Their words would ride on the wind from the cotton fields.

> *When Israel was in Egypt's land*
> *Let my people go*
> *Oppressed so hard, they could not stand*

47

Let my people go.
God said to go down
Go down Brother Moses
Brother Moses
To the shore of the great Nile River.
Go to Egypt.
Go to Egypt.
Tell Pharaoh
Let my people go.
Yes, my God is a mighty God
Lord, deliver
And he set old Israel free
Swallowed the Egyptian Army
Lord, Deliver
with the waves of the great Red Sea.

The musical pleas and the blended harmony of the many voices drifted in on cascades of sounds. The echoing melodies and chords, washing over the slaves, would curdle Lovey's blood with the song's plaintive quality. In spite of the sorrow conveyed on the wind, Lovey sensed a unity between the men and women. As young as she was, she also intuited that there had to be a certain amount of comfort in each other's arms. She didn't know about love yet, but figured that two could soften some of slavery's fiery lashes better than one.

The first time Lovey heard someone call her "Buck Head," she didn't know that the name referred to the white blood in her veins. When her little girl friend, Letha, told her what it meant, Lovey made a silent vow. She'd sworn she'd never be a "white man's slop jar." Although she loved her mother, she would always harbor mixed feelings of distaste and blame for Oriole.

Try as as she would, she could never quite forgive Oriole for having had children by a white man—even when she was grown enough to understand that her mother had never had any choice in the matter. Living on the fringes of the slave community as her little family unit did, Lovey had been a precocious little girl. That was why she had already picked out her husband by the time she was nine years old.

Lovey had her eye on old Black Noble from the time she first began noticing the special glisten of sweat on his ebony back. She was a little girl picking tobacco and hoeing jimpson weeds in the alley row behind Noble. As the lead row slave, Noble could pick more cotton or tobacco than anyone. Although she knew at the age of nine that she couldn't be considered for a mate for Noble, she knew that later, perhaps at thirteen or fourteen, they could "jump the broom" or even legally marry, since they were free.

What had also attracted Lovey to Noble Hightower was the knowledge that he came from an old slave family with history. The Hightowers were three generations of blood-related Blacks who had never been separated or sold from the plantation during slavery. After Emancipation, the former slaves had agreed with the Master to continue to work the land for pay, until they could afford to buy some back. They never believed in the forty acres and a mule promise. With rare exceptions, the Hightowers were all obsidian Black—as close to full-blooded African as former slaves could get. They were proud of their purity, claiming they had never been intermingled or bred with any other race of slaves. They exuded a smug superiority—generally only reserved for the "house niggers"—which surpassed that of the mulattos. Because they loved being close to the earth and working the land, the Hightowers boasted that they were proud to be field hands. They swore that one day they were going to own some of that very land. "A hoe Negro I was born, and a hoe Negro I'm going to die," was their motto. "We come from the mother earth, and we can be free as long as we stay close to the earth."

Nurturing this thought in their bosoms had nursed them through two hundred years of captivity. Wrenched from the earth's dark bowels, the motherland, the Hightowers had remained a free people because of their affinity with the land. Anything they touched, they could make grow. That was why, after she entered into legal marriage with Noble Hightower at fourteen, Lovey was not surprised how easily she bore him eighteen living children in quick succession. Jewel's mother, Luralee, had been the thirteenth living child of the siblingship. All of the children had been born at home, and Lovey had never lost a baby.

Although she had been raised by her grandparents from infancy until she was eleven years old, Jewel only knew bits and pieces, like a patch work quilt, about Mama Lovey's life. By the time Jewel was even born, most of Lovey's older children had left home, spreading to the four winds, some never to return. As a child, Jewel only personally knew Uncle Soap, Uncle Buddy, Uncle Cash, Aunt Illy, Aunt Mercy D, Aunt Sukey, Aunt Beulah, and Aunt Sunday. Because her parents separated when she was only a year of age, Jewel had never met her own father, Eli Johnson. Everyone always said her parents broke up because Luralee had wanted to leave Mansfield, Louisiana and relocate to Tulsa, Oklahoma. Later, Luralee had claimed that she left her husband because he hadn't wanted to move up in the world. But that wasn't the sole reason that Luralee had left her   husband at a time when divorce and separation were rare events. Luralee had been a woman born ahead of her time. She'd silently promised herself when she was a child having to share one banana with five brothers and sisters that she was not going to have a "houseful of babies" like her mother, Lovey, had shamelessly done.

Regardless of the reason handed down in the family archives, Luralee was also a woman born ahead of, yet shaped by, her times. Marcus Garvey, the West Indian, had founded the Universal Negro Improvement Association, heralding Blacks to move back to Africa. Ragtime greats such as Eubie, along with Noble Sissle, painted the world ablaze with rhythm and syncopated sound. She intuitively understood what Eubie meant by "You gotta get the gettin' while the gettin' is good." From her confining marriage, Luralee heard the clarion cry of progress, and her heels did not want to miss the boat.

Depositing her children—Jewel, along with her baby brother, Bubba—in rural Vernon, Oklahoma, with no more fanfare than one would drop off a sack of potatoes, Luralee went to work in Tulsa, Oklahoma as a live-in domestic for a white woman. Throughout the Depression, Luralee sent silver dollars home to all of her family members. In the meantime, Mama Lovey and Papa raised up her children.

No matter how much Mama Lovey and Papa tried to give Jewel love, she had always felt that she missed out on something important during her formative years. That something was a mother's love. As far as she was concerned, she had never known a mother's love. Not the way that she had wanted and needed love. Not the way she had sworn she'd love her babies one day when she had her own.

When Jewel was eleven, Mama Lovey and Papa died within months of each other. After the grandparents' death, Jewel and her brother, Bubba, were first farmed out to live with Aunt Beulah and her husband, Uncle Thed. Uncle Thed was a preacher at the Grover Lane Church. He and Aunt Beulah had three children, Walline, Zenola, and Thed Junior, whom everyone called "Son." As crazy as Jewel was about her cousins, she tried to stay out of Aunt Beulah's way.

"It's a shame that Sister don't raise her own children," Aunt Beulah often told Aunt Sukey, when they thought Jewel wasn't listening. They called her mother "Sister."

"She too busy up in the city trying to buy up all those houses." Aunt Sukey always picked up the shuttle of conversation and ran with it.

"Yeah, she send money to everybody each month," Aunt Beulah continued. "Just showing off. Money ain't everything."

"Think she something. I'm the one here washing her kids' clothes and feeding them. That little bit she sending me hardly feed a growing girl like Jewel."

As they wove their threnody of scorn and spite, Jewel's hands kept moving. She swept the yard, carried water from the well, and worked in the fields. Whenever she became tired, Jewel thought of how hard Papa said he used to work in the fields as a little boy during and after slavery. Just the thought would keep her going.

Mama Lovey and Papa had been old when Jewel stayed with them. From watching their hushed-mouth ways, Jewel learned to say some and hold some back. By the time Jewel came to live with her grandparents, they had seen enough of life to know they were tired and had nothing else to say about the matter.

Until Jewel lived with Aunt Beulah and her family, the child had never realized how quiet Mama Lovey and Papa's house had been. In a young household, Jewel was startled, at first, by how lively and noisy the children were. She peeked out of the corner of her eyes as Uncle Thed kissed Aunt Beulah. She furtively studied that special look that would pass between the couple some nights before they sent the children to bed early. Jewel had never witnessed any outward show of affection between Mama Lovey and Papa. She never once saw Mama Lovey or Papa touch each other, let alone kiss one another. Both grandparents had lavished what was left of their spent love on the two grandchildren, yet, after a lifetime of living together, they seemed to have nothing left for each other. Jewel used to wonder how they had even made eighteen babies together.

Under Aunt Beulah's tutelage, the main lesson Jewel had learned was that boy children were superior to girl children. Aunt Beulah made such a difference in Thed Junior that for the longest, Jewel thought she was saying "Sun" when she called Thed Junior, "Son." Honey dripped off that word like a smoked cone when it came out of Aunt Beulah's mouth.

"This piece of cherry pie is for Son," Aunt Beulah always made a point of telling Jewel.

Jewel learned to look on as her cousins ate freely. Meanwhile, she had to ask and better not ask too often. At night, through the walls, she'd hear Aunt Beulah munching on nuts under the covers. Although she never was caught, Jewel began to steal food for herself and

Bubba after a while. When the kerosene lamp went out, she learned to smuggle it to their bedroom.

Nonetheless, regardless of how Jewel tried not to risk incurring the wrath of Aunt Beulah, she failed. She didn't realize that the budding breasts under her chemise and the beginning woman curves made Aunt Beulah uneasy.

If Jewel ever tried to play with the other children, chasing squirrels or playing "Ring around the Rosy," Beulah somehow found work for her.

"Go pick those cucumbers, Jewel Mae," Beulah often snapped for no apparent reason.

Not knowing what was wrong, but well understanding the meaning through the tone of voice, Jewel obeyed.

To keep from crying, Jewel liked to think of Papa whenever her hands were in soil.

"This is Hightower land, Jewel Mae." Papa loved to brag on their land. "The Hightowers were the first of the freedman in this area to buy and own land in Louisiana and now in Vernon, Oklahoma."

Jewel had heard it whispered among the aunts that Oriole, the great-grandmother whom the child had never seen, since she died before the turn of the century, had been the reason the Hightowers had so much land. From what her aunts whispered, Jewel gathered that Oriole had been the Master's mistress. Even if he had possessed an inclination to, the Master could never have married Oriole.

But he had given her children—his children, although no one ever acknowledged the fact openly— hundreds of acres of land. They said that this white man had gone so far as to send his son, Caleb, North to be educated. This distant relative—this great-uncle Caleb—was said to be so light, he could pass for a white man. And did.

It was rumored that he was a rich Realtor in Chicago somewhere, but he wouldn't speak to his own family, even if he passed them on the streets.

When Scooter, Beulah's youngest child was born, Jewel was given so much of the responsibility, she felt just as if he was her own baby.

"Look at her," Aunt Sukey commented to Beulah one day. "Walking around with that baby hitched to her hip just like he was hers."

"Sure didn't get that from Luralee. She's a natural-born mother. Just like Mama Lovey. That Sister of ours though. Hmph. A cow got more love for a heifer than Luralee got for those kids of hers," Aunt Beulah remarked.

It always bothered Jewel to hear them talk about her mother, Luralee, but she didn't know why. She really didn't know her mother, only seeing her once a month sometimes. So when Luralee landed in her life again, Jewel's thirteen-year-old world capsized. Without warning or explanation, she and Bubba were uprooted like tumbleweed and plopped down with Luralee and her new husband, Zach. Jewel was so heartbroken over leaving Scooter, her little cousin whom she'd had almost sole responsibility for for two years, that she cried for days. Scooter and she had become inseparable. While Beulah and the others worked in the fields, he had been her little shadow.

Although Jewel never believed it, Luralee was not so unfeeling as to be blind to the girl's pain. Whether people believed it or not, Luralee had not left her children because she didn't care. As the child of former slaves, she had received so little emotionally and physically that there was a part of her spirit that would always remain restless and in need of more. She had never wanted her children to grow up in the country. Contrary to what anyone said or believed, Luralee had left her children so that she could give them a chance at a better life. Unfortunately, it had taken Luralee twelve years to get herself together and gather her children back to her bosom in the city of Tulsa.

To soften some of Jewel's anguish, Luralee had even bought Jewel a doll. This was Jewel's first doll. The doll had been white, with a round ceramic head and painted cornflower-blue eyes.

Although Jewel kept the doll with her, even after she was grown up and left home, its arrival was a bit late in her life. This was her first doll that wasn't made from a corncob, but by then, Jewel was a half-grown, bloodletting woman.

The other presence that softened some of the topsy-turvyness of her young, unanchored life was the meeting of Solomon. Jewel had experienced several schoolgirl crushes, but she fell in love with the flame that was a fifteen-year-old Solomon Shepherd, her newspaper boy.

Last, Luralee had re-enrolled Jewel in school. She was only placed one year behind to make up for the two years she had missed school while staying with Beulah. One day after school, Solly had carried Jewel's books home for her. He got up the nerve to talk to Luralee.

"Ma'am," he said to Luralee, "can I take Jewel to the movies? I'll have her back by nine."

"Who all going with y'all?" Luralee asked.

"My sister and her boyfriend going."

"All right." Although Luralee consented, she started preaching to Jewel, as soon as Solly left.

"Don't let that little darkie get up under your dress, you hear me, Jewel."

"Mama, he's not like that."

"Look, they all start out looking innocent before they get the goods under the hood. I hear his Daddy, who's supposed to be a preacher, is a killer diller."

Jewel was quiet. She never said much to Luralee, because she didn't know how to take her. Sometimes, she wondered how a mother and daughter could be so different. It seemed as though Luralee had sailed back into her life with little or no regret for having left her children in the first place.

Luralee continued. "You don't want to get stood up in the Chastisement Corner, do you? And with that no-good husband of Beulah's—got the nerve to be a preacher--that would be good as he want. I can see him now, standing you up in the Chastisement Corner. He never forgave me for taking y'all back. That was extra money for his don't-want-to-work, jackleg, preaching time."

"Please, Mama."

"Don't please me, Miss Ma'am. You think I didn't see how they was working you to death. You nearly all but suckled that last baby of theirs."

Luralee just didn't know. Jewel did not need to be reminded of the one or two unfortunate girls who came up pregnant without a husband. Their lives were "ruint" forever.

"She ruint," people said about the girls who had to drop out of high school in disgrace. If the boy wouldn't marry her, her life was doubly ruint.

To add lime to the open wound of public disgrace, the girls had to stand up in the Chastisement Corner in Uncle Thed's church at Grover Lane Baptist. Then, the girls had to face the entire congregation, hang their heads, and say, "I repent." Even so, most of the girls refused to name their baby's father.

Although Luralee didn't smoke, drink, or party, she was not a person taken with organized religion. She felt that the church was full of hypocrites, and she always said that she didn't particularly feel like sharing company with them on the few off days she had, anyway.

But whenever Luralee witnessed a chastisement, she'd become fired up with indignation.

"Probably one of the deacon's babies, anyway," Luralee grumbled one Sunday after church. "I ain't never seen no girl get in trouble by herself yet. Takes two. The girl always left holding the bag. Makes me sick, talking about the children is illegitimate. Wasn't nobody worried about folks getting married during slavery. The more babies the better. Folks didn't care if you had a baby by a different man every year, long as you was breaking your back for the white man."

Jewel remained quiet. She never knew what to say to Luralee.

"And that Solly, you watch that boy," Luralee rambled on. "Y'all was sitting awfully close on that swing the other night. You sure don't want to have no baby by somebody that dark. I don't see what you see in him, no way. He's black as tar baby. But you just like Mama. Love you some Black man. I guess you can't help yourself. It's in your blood. Your daddy, Elija, was dark as a Nigger-toe nut. Midnight black, he was.

"Quiet as it's kept, your Aunt Illy, Aunt Sunday — well all my sisters in fact — are married to dark-skinned men. I guess it's in all of our blood. Papa was jet black, light as Mama was. Come to think of it, everybody else is trying to lighten up their family, but we the onliest ones trying to go back to Africa."

The only advice Luralee ever gave Jewel regarding birth control was, "Keep your panties up and your dress tail down."

Well, for three years, Jewel obeyed Luralee. But young hot blood being what it is, Solly and Jewel discovered a lot of kissing and loving which could be accomplished in those two boundaries.

Like amber honey dripping out of a beehive, like the wind somersaulting in the leaves of trees, like smoke hickory chips on an autumn day, intimacy with Solly was as inevitable as nature.

Jewel graduated from high school, turned nineteen, and married Solly all within twenty-four hours.

Six months later, when Solomon Junior was born, Jewel had been ecstatic. She had been happy from the time she found out she was pregnant with Cake Sandwich.

She just knew she was going to have a boy. And she didn't care if her sin went against the grain of Mama Lovey's Bible teachings. She was finally going to have a real family.

From the time Jewel laid eyes on her new son, she'd thought Solomon Junior was the most beautiful baby she'd ever seen. Although Jewel was what people called "canary-yellow," she loved having a little hazel-nut baby boy more than if he'd been light-skinned.

When Luralee urged her to pinch the baby's pug nose or to rub cocoa butter into his sable skin, Jewel turned a deaf ear to the old wives' tales. In spite of the fact that Solly Junior always held a special place in her heart being her first-born, she never made a difference in any of her subsequent dark babies. If there was a favoring towards her children, it was not along color lines. Unlike many fair-complected Negro women during the forties who were the mothers of dark-skinned children, Jewel did not subscribe to this particular ingrained insanity carried over from slavery.

Jewel's favoring towards her children was always towards her boys. She just couldn't seem to help herself. That was all she had ever seen were women making over their male children.

Out of Mama Lovey's eighteen, she always heard her say, "Boys are important to a woman. They can be somebody in life. Take care of you in your old life. But a girl. Bahh Jesus — a girl. A girl is a split-tail just born for pain and suffering."

Mama Lovey had lost one daughter, Mina, who was eighteen at the time of her death. She had died from diphtheria. The only time Jewel ever heard Lovey mention this long-deceased daughter was in connection to her sons. "Thank God, it wasn't one of my boys."

Jewel had watched the way Aunt Beulah made over Thed, Junior. "Son-this, Son-that."

But the crowning lesson had been watching Luralee. Wasn't the way her mother, Luralee, treated her proof that a boy child was more special? It was as if the twelve-year separation from her children had never

The Ebony Tree

existed between Bubba and Luralee, they were so close. Even after Bubba married, he chose to settle in Tulsa, so that he could be near Luralee. He worked as a shoe salesperson during the day and visited his mother every night.

Although Jewel hadn't wanted to live with her in-laws, she had been happy to be a new wife and mother. She finally had a real family. This baby was hers, and no one could take him from her like they had taken Scooter.

62

It all started back with Miss Trudy in the 1920's, Jewel decided. At any rate, her mother, Luralee, had believed in it, so much so that she made her own potion called "Blue Grease" to ward off all evil spirits and spells. Moreover, Luralee touted that "Blue Grease" had other medicinal properties. It was a cure-all for the gout, the misery, and anything else that ailed you. "She's been fixed," Luralee used to tell Jewel, whenever she pointed to a demented woman. "Don't ever leave your hair laying around or eat from anybody."

Jewel's first knowledge of women putting hexes on the wives of their married lovers started when she was a child, living with Mama Lovey and Papa. Whether Jewel ever talked about it or not, she believed in it, too. In any case, Jewel remained encysted in her house, without concern for socializing. Besides, she never wanted any woman in her house ogling at Solly. Her attitude was that he could get in enough trouble on his own. Why would she bring temptation to him on a silver platter? For that reason, Jewel wore the world like a loose-fitting garment.

Jewel would never forget the night that she'd first seen it in action in Delray. She'd just gotten the last of her children bathed and settled down for bed, when a knock came at the door. It was Syreeta, Amanda Green's oldest daughter.

"What is it?" Jewel asked, when she saw the girl's terrified face.

"Come quick!" Syreeta pleaded. "It's Mama! I don't know what's wrong with her."

"What do you mean?"

"She's been beating on all of us. She won't sleep. She's talking all out of her head."

"Watch the kids, Solly." Jewel grabbed up her sweater.

The sky was the color of the indigo dye Mama Lovey used to make. The crescent moon overhead shed only a machete of light. Because the two women both lived near the middle of the street, and the street lamps were only at both ends, their globes did little to brighten Jewel's path. The night air, still redolent with the smell of burnt leaves, made Jewel nauseous.

In the evening, everyone burnt their trash and leaves in the back alley, making the street reek of smoke. At the time, Jewel hadn't known that her queasy stomach was caused by more than just the wind. Suddenly, the wind began to rise until it crescendoed, howling like a deranged and jilted lover through the Dutch elms that lined Cottrow Street. Jewel's skin prickled up with foreboding. Fear oozed from her pores, causing her to break into a cold sweat. Rushing down the six houses, she shivered. As soon as Jewel saw Amanda, she knew what was wrong with her.

If she hadn't seen it with her own eyes as a child, she wouldn't have believed it herself. Her grandmother, Mama Lovey, once drank some cow's milk that Papa had brought home. Later on, the family found out that the milk had come from Miss Trudy's, whom they all knew was Papa's outside woman. After that, it seemed that every time Mama Lovey would hang up clothes on the line, she'd bark like a dog. She began to throw up a green bile-looking substance. Formerly a big, foreboding woman, Mama Lovey began to waste away. Everyone said she would have died had not her older daughter, Illy, come to visit. Illy took one look at Mama Lovey and she knew what was wrong. She told Papa that she was taking Lovey home with her to "rest awhile." Papa didn't say anything. He just figured this was the cure for most of the women in the family when they went through "the change of life" and "went haywire." Papa never knew that Illy took Mama Lovey to a voodoo doctor over in New Orleans.

Whatever the voodoo doctor did, it drove the evil spirit out of Lovey. They say she vomited up frogs when the antidote began to work. After that Mama Lovey returned home and to her old self. She was just quieter. And she never drank or ate anything else Papa brought home.

"Don't you eat for or from anybody, Jewel Mae," Mama Lovey always said after that. "Don't leave any hair laying around. Take your hair and burn it at sundown. And don't throw no hair out when the wind is blowing from the North to the South. And you don't sweep hair out when the sun is setting in the west."

Looking at Amanda, now, Jewel knew that Miss Mamie was about as close to a voodoo doctor as anything Delray had ever had.

"You need to go see Miss Mamie," she said to Amanda.

"It's not true. Not true," Amanda kept repeating over and over. Amanda started tearing at her clothes. "I see snakes crawling all over me. I've got a smell on me."

"I don't smell anything, Amanda," Jewel told her neighbor.

"They're talking to me. They're all over at the window talking to me."

"Syreeta, go get your mother some milk and warm it up," Jewel said, turning to the daughter, hanging in the doorway. Syreeta looked as frightened as a cat with its back arched and its fur standing on end.

"I don't know what's wrong with her," Tommy Lee, her husband, said quietly. Jewel looked up from her neighbor, whom she was trying to urge into bed. She had not noticed Tommy Lee, who had come to stand in the doorway. He looked too nervous to enter into the bedroom. As if crossing the very threshold would contaminate him. As if whatever Amanda had was contagious.

"Just like men. Leave all the dirty work up to women," Jewel thought. "Like he doesn't know what's wrong with her. Like he ain't behind whatever is the thing that pushed her right over the edge."

Jewel gave Tommy Lee a long baleful stare, then turned away. *But for the grace of God, go I,* she mused. *If I would allow it, Solly would have me howling at the moon, too.*

Finally, Jewel had gotten Amanda to bed, with the promise that the latter would try to sleep. That night, after Jewel had gone home, they said that Amanda tried to kill herself. Tried to put her head in the gas stove oven. Tommy Lee had her committed to the state hospital for the mentally insane the next day. Amanda remained there for the rest of her natural life. Her oldest daughter, Syreeta, had to finish raising her other four children.

Later, Jewel learned what had happened to Amanda. Everyone in Delray knew that Amanda grew the most beautiful roses in the neighborhood. Every day she ambled over to the row of rosebushes just to admire her and God's handiwork.

For fun, she liked to sniff the pollen, even talk to the roses. A well-worn trail ran in Amanda's front yard and led directly from the porch to the rose bushes. Amanda's roses lent color to an otherwise drab yard and street. The riot of yellow, red, white and pink roses lit the yard up in the spring, and perfumed the air with their dying breath in the fall. This one little indulgence was enough to set the serpent of envy slithering outside of Amanda's little garden of Eden.

One Sunday, while Tommy Lee and Amanda were driving to church in their old Nash, they saw a neighbor named Donna Joe walking in the same direction. When they saw she was headed to the same destination, they offered Donna Joe a ride to church. Unbeknown to Amanda, Donna Joe had a hankering for Tommy Lee for years. On the drive to church, Amanda's silver comb, an ornament which had been an heirloom in her family for years, slipped out of her hair and into the back seat. The comb was never to be seen again.

Later, the hawk bird of rumor had it that Donna Joe was the one who had slipped the comb into her purse. They said that she had taken a piece of hair that she retrieved from the comb to a root woman. They said it wasn't Miss Mamie, because she generally worked in good human affairs and not in evil curses. Whoever the conjurer was placed a curse on Amanda, working through her strand of hair. Donna Joe was able to activate the curse by planting the hair along the usual path that Amanda always traveled to accomplish her daily ritual of smelling her roses. Within days, Amanda began to deteriorate. First, she became restless. They say she became increasingly irritable and was unable to sleep at night. She'd always been a mild-mannered mother, so when she began beating on her children, they hadn't known what to think or make of it. By the time Syreeta came and asked Jewel for help, Amanda was too far gone. The voodoo had made inroads into her spirit in a way she could not cast off or undo.

Like most people raised in the country, Jewel believed in spirits. She also believed in dream books and hitting the numbers. The number business in Delray was a small quasi-legal racket. Miss Mamie was one of the main collectors for this pipe dream. Whenever Jewel dreamed about Papa or Mama Lovey, she played straight 777 out of her dream book. Although she never hit the number for the type of money that could move her family out of Delray, Jewel was able to get little hits here and there. Once, she was able to fix the furnace and another time she was able to get coal for the winter with her winnings. By the time Jewel found out that she was pregnant with her sixth child, she was already starting to show. Just as with her last several pregnancies, Solly was beginning to stay out later and later. Nothing made Jewel more miserable than being pregnant and sitting home alone, manless, night after night, while Solly cavorted with the neighborhood bad women. Probably Eldoretha Gray.

In spite of all Solly had done to hurt and disappoint Jewel, their bedroom was still the one arena of her life which was a field of buttercups to romp and play in. Nothing made Jewel more miserable and drove her crazier than being pregnant and laying up as dry as a desert, alone in her bed, while Solly was out oiling up someone else.

Jewel did something she'd never done before. She made a trip to Miss Mamie's when she was six months pregnant. Miss Mamie looked surprised to see her again. She lifted her furry eyebrows.

"It's not about the baby," Jewel assured her.

"How's the little critter coming along?"

"It's moving around a lot. I guess it will be all right."

"Hmmmph. Any time a colored baby catch hold to life, it's hard to get rid of them. How you think we survived slavery working out in the fields while we was pregnant?"

Jewel was impatient and wanted to get to the point of her visit, but she felt like it was time to be quiet. She nodded her head and said, "Ha'mercy."

"Yes, my Grandma Phoebe was one hundred and eight years old when she died. Before she died she could tell you some stories make your head turn white. Back in slavery, the master could have a colored man's wife while he had to wait outside."

"Ha'mercy."

"A woman never knew if her child was gon' come here black or white. One man killed the little albino-looking baby his wife had on her plantation, and they burned him alive. Said you could hear his screams for miles around."

"Mmmm, mmmmmm, mmmmm."

The two women fell silent, absorbed in another world.

Jewel was thinking about how she was not worried in the least that the baby she was carrying was Solly's. Her only concern was if she could just get all of them up and out of the way before she started over with another baby! If she just didn't love them so hard, maybe it wouldn't matter. But she ached every time she thought of the advantages she saw in white magazines that she wanted to give to her children. Coming out parties. Camping trips. Music lessons.

Jewel wondered what that had to be like. Living with your husband and pregnant for another man—a white man at that. Jewel prided herself on having a good reputation and being "a good woman." In Delray, she'd heard of several married women with rather unsavory backgrounds who ran around more openly than the men did. Jewel was no longer the innocent country girl she'd been when she first moved to the North. Still, she couldn't fathom how it was done. Sleeping with two men at the same time. Lord, her grandfather, Papa, womanizer that he was, would turn in his grave if he knew of such carrying-ons they had up here in the North.

Jewel remembered when her neighbor, Matilda, had given birth to an alabaster-skinned, blue-eyed baby—what with she and her husband, J.B., both the color of a black walnut tree. Jewel could hear the cussing and hollering and pleading going on for days over the back fence.

"It reached back to the ancestors!" Matilda would cry over and over.

Slap! Whop! Bam! Another slap! No one ever heard it mentioned again, but later, the little pale-milk child was often seen playing outside with all the hickory-hued brothers and sisters.

"Tell me," Miss Mamie said, causing Jewel to start, "what did you come to see me for?"

"I want my husband to come home at night," Jewel said, slipping a folded bill into Miss Mamie's biscuit-colored palm.

"Have you looked at his feet? Are they real black on the bottom?"

"Come to think of it, they are."

"How about his big right toe? Is it real black and crusty?"

"I don't know."

"Well, look at it when you catch him sleeping. And when he pees, pour salt down the toilet."

Miss Mamie went to her kitchen cabinet and mixed together two white powders.

"Sprinkle this in front of your door whenever your man leaves. Put a little in the corners of your house. This will ward off traveling feet."

Miss Mamie also handed Jewel a bottle of Water of Notre Dame.

"When you mop and clean, use this. It will bring peace in your home," she said to Jewel.

It seemed to Jewel that for the rest of her pregnancy, Solly came home early and in a loving mood. He was somewhat puzzled himself, knowing how he loved to run the streets while Jewel was pregnant.

When Midge was a child, she never thought that it was strange that she didn't have a picture of what she looked like in the mirror of her mind. Although there were only several family portraits, in which she was always smiling widely — clearly a happy child — there was no picture or self-image housed inside Midge's soul at all when she was growing up. All she knew was that she had two older and two younger brothers. She also intuitively understood that she was part of the glue that held together this group of human beings called family. She folded and ironed shirts for the older two brothers. She gave bottles to the younger two brothers. As the oldest girl, Midge cooked as soon as she could pull a chair up to the stove. She carried babies slung on her hips from the time she could remember. Sometimes, accompanied by Cake Sandwich and Judge, Midge even went to pay the light, gas, or water bill for Jewel. Although they never had any of their utilities cut off, Midge wondered why her mother wrung her hands each month as to how they would pay them. One day flowed pretty much as the next for Midge until a change came into her life, upsetting her seven-year-old world like a glass of milk spilled accidentally at the dinner table.

This distinctive day punctuated the cotton-candy nebula of her entire childhood. Midge remembered that it came about the spring after the first day it snowed. That time — that afternoon a long, long time ago — when it had snowed for the first time that winter.

Midge measured time in birthdays, Christmases, and first snows. So she still remembered the time Mama had left her in charge like a big girl to watch her brothers.

But now time had become her enemy. Mama had disappeared! She had been gone for what seemed like forever. The sun had flung open a whole lot of new days. The moon had winked at several nights. Where was Mama? No one ever bothered to tell the child where Mama had disappeared to, and if, at all, she would ever return. Midge's worse fears had been realized. Mama had run away from home.

Midge was so despondent, she drooped around for four days. What would she do? How would she make it? Miss Sylvester, the fat lady who rented one of the rooms upstairs, had been watching the children. Studying Miss Sylvester out of the corners of her eyes, Midge watched the fat lady dip snuff, chew the wad of tobacco, and spit it in a lard can. Midge trembled. Miss Sylvester had two braided horns in front of her ears and two behind them. To Midge, she looked like a bull who was ready to charge at any moment. Miss Sylvester hardly got up from the chair in the kitchen. As she leaned back in one of the chairs—one of the few with a back on it—she seemed to direct all activity from a supine position. With one arm resting on her round pot belly, she kept the other arm and hand free to dip corn bread into a glass of buttermilk. Or when she wasn't eating, she was sucking on tobacco. Finally, Midge couldn't take any more of the mystery.

Arms akimbo, feet planted firmly on the floor before Miss Sylvester's shrine of adulthood, Midge demanded,

"When my Mama coming home?"

"She'll be here soon," Sylvester told her. Children were only to be seen, not heard.

A few minutes later, Midge heard her tell Judge and Cake Sandwich, "Your grandma gon' be here directly."

But where was Mama?

Several more hours crept by. Out of nowhere, Mama came walking through the front door. Daddy was with her. Mama carried a tiny bundle in a white blanket. Midge recognized the white blanket right away. It was the same blanket in which Mama had brought Baby Boy and Joey home from the hospital. So this was what all the whispering and the secrecy had been about. Mama had a new baby!

"Yay! Mama's home!" Cake Sandwich clamored.

Joey and Baby Boy began to whimper, hoping Mama could see how neglected and lost they had been without the sun of her presence.

Jewel leaned over and kissed her two baby boys. She was so weak, she felt the walls sway, but she had to hold herself up. She could already see how her house had come apart. And her children looked so throwed-away, she could cry.

"Can I see my baby sis-sister?" Judge stammered. He stood on his tiptoes, trying to peer inside of the little bundle.

"She's so pretty, Mama," Cake Sandwich cooed. "She's little."

Judge cheered, "Yay! We got a new ba-bbba-by sis-sister!"

Midge was the only one who didn't comment. She felt like she'd just been run over by a street car. She had to think. Why hadn't anyone told her? Or had they told her and it failed to register? She was so used to baby brothers, she was dumbfounded. A cold glass of water in the face, it was! Midge dissembled the muscles in her face into the amiable facade she always presented to Jewel.

74

"Mama, can I change your baby?"

As Jewel laid the baby down on the bed, Midge watched under surreptitious eyelashes.

"Wait until she gets a little older," Mama was murmuring.

Watching Mama unwrap the blanket, then change the cloth diaper, slyness and envy edged into Midge's little heart. There was no little penis spraying in her face under that diaper. Only a vulva, as smooth as a banana skin. So it was true! It was a girl baby! A sister!

Suddenly, Midge felt the ground beneath her shift. She'd no longer be "the only gal baby." Was that what Daddy had been trying to tell her in his cockeye-mamied fashion?

Without warning or explanation, her world capsized. Everything would change. She didn't know how, but she knew that things would be different.

Although she suffered the brunt of much of Jewel's frustration, Midge had already come to recognize her power in a houseful of boys. She had talked before either of her older brothers, therefore, she was often the spokesperson. Like the time Cake Sandwich got into Daddy's whiskey and overdosed. It was Midge, who at two, was able to explain what was wrong with him, so that their parents were able to rush Cake Sandwich to the hospital in the nick of time.

Midge had always been like the queen, making decisions, chastising all the boys, and giving orders like a drill sergeant. Now, she didn't know what to expect.

Midge was eight years old the first time she considered "offing" her little sister. Midge often went walking "the latest addition to the family" up and down Cottrow Street. Midge did this in an effort to give Jewel a break. She was so afraid for how fragile her mother appeared after the new baby's birth, she was hypervigilant at all times.

Oh please don't run off and leave us again, Midge prayed every day. Thus, she tried to be "a good little girl."

Because she tried to anticipate Jewel's needs, Midge learned her mother's schedule by heart. With Midge's help, Jewel washed all the clothes every Monday. Tuesdays were the days Jewel reserved for ironing all the clothes, including the sheets and pillow cases. Generally, Jewel sprinkled the clothes with water, rolled them into a bundle and put them into her deep freezer. Sometimes, after she boiled it to a creamy consistency, she used Argo starch to iron her clothes into a stiff professional look. Every Wednesday, Jewel beat her rugs on the clothing line or stretched out her curtains on a wood rack to let them air dry in the sun.

Thursdays, Midge helped Jewel polish her maple furniture in the living room. On Friday, Jewel got on her hands and knees to scrub the kitchen floor. Afterwards, the older three children would help her apply Aero wax on the floors. To polish the linoleum floors, the children slid around in their bare socks. This worked out fine for all concerned. The children got to pretend they were ice skating, and Jewel discovered a way to keep her floors shiny. On Saturday, Jewel gave the children Father John's and Castor Oil before they went to bed. On Sunday — if Jewel could make it — she went to the African Methodist Church. She picked this church, because it was more conservative than the other Negro Church, Zion Baptist.

More often than not, Jewel just slicked up her

children and sent them to Sunday School. Jewel's hands moved from the time she got up and stoked the coals in the furnace, until she kissed the last sleepy head on a pillow.

Everyone — including her relatives — always said that Jewel kept a clean house. The mark of "keeping house" in Delray was having more than five children and not having a house that reeked of urine.

Although Judge wet the bed every night, Jewel aired his mattress every week and used a yellow rubber sheet under his covers.

It was such a busy schedule, Jewel failed to notice that Midge and Cake Sandwich resented going to pay the light and gas bill. Solly and his brother, A.J, usually hung up Jewel's laundry when she was pregnant. With the exception of her pregnancies, Jewel, with a little help from Midge, did all the housework and most of the gardening.

The particular day that Midge first began contemplating mayhem towards her little sister began one summer day the following year. Midge, in an effort to give Jewel a break, was pushing the well-worn stroller down the street, when she passed a widowed neighbor, Mrs. Pearson.

After the proper cordialities, Mrs. Pearson took the liberty to step away from the bush of azaleas she was trimming, to amble off her porch, and to block Midge's path on the sidewalk. Without asking, she pulled back the blanket off the baby's face.

"Oh, I see your little sister got the looks in the family. She looks like your mother," Mrs. Pearson pronounced.

A jaundice began to creep inside of Midge, bathing her over with hate. Everyone always said she looked like her Daddy? Was that bad? By the time Midge made it to Miss Coretta's store, a half-baked plot had hatched in her head.

What if she accidentally lost the baby? Would Mama believe it? Or what if she let the stroller just kind of mosey out in the street when a car was speeding up it?

So, while Midge ran inside the store to get milk for the family, since they had drunk up all the milk left by the milk wagon, she carelessly left the stroller in the street by the curb. But somehow, the hand of reason made her run back and retrieve the stroller. Still, she told herself, "No, she's not prettier than me. Where? She doesn't look like Mama. I know what I'll do. I'll tell her she's ugly."

And ugly was just how Midge and her little sister felt for years. The nucleus where the self should have developed failed to germinate in both girls. For Midge, she had been raised on the idea that a colored Prince Charming—somehow imbued with the qualities of the white faces of her dreams—would come along and save the day. She was told to expect nothing more than a husband. A home. And children. The problem, for Midge, began when she started to want more.

"**W**hy you stay with Daddy?" Jewel's boys used to ask her when they were small. Jewel never answered. Yet, in spite of her silence, the deep sighs that escaped whenever she rolled out apple pie crusts, or the vehement hisses she made when she looked out the window, waiting for Solly, cried out in every corner of the house. Sometimes, Jewel looked so lost, her boys tried to cheer her up. The boys knew how to tell jokes to make her laugh. To make up for Solly's lapses, the boys would even bring her scrawny dandelions. They blew the spores away when they died, reminding Jewel of the same joy of discovery she had known years ago.

Besides, dandelions soothed Jewel. When she was a child, she'd grown up thinking dandelion soup was the best dish in the world. She hadn't realized that there was a Depression going on out in the world, and that dandelion soup was not a delicacy.

But Midge. . . .Now, Midge was another story. She was so taken with her father, she was a grown woman before she ever asked that question.

Midge was a Daddy's girl, plain and simple. Whenever Solly had a hangover, it was Midge who took him his coffee. Midge who poured it in the saucer and helped him blow the liquid so it would not burn his tongue.

"Just like your Daddy," Jewel used to growl whenever she was mad at Solly and had reason—or no reason—to punish Midge. Because Jewel was often an inconsistent disciplinarian, she did not use a lot of inconsistent disciplinarian, she did not use a lot of spanking, so Midge was spared any physical scars. Their battles were all invisible and waged in an emotional arena.

Living with Solly had inevitably wrought changes in Jewel's once soft-spoken personality. A carapace developed where her heart used to have soft spots in it. Sometimes, Jewel looked in the mirror and wondered who the haggard woman she saw reflected back was. What scared her most was the hardness around her eyes. The tight grip of poverty, the stranglehold of want, and the constant onslaught of need wore Jewel down. Plum wore her out. Life was always fraught with uncertainty, worry, and chaos. For Jewel, "the poor house" and "outdoors" were the modern-day replacements of the bloodhounds chasing the runaway slaves. Their ever-present, fiery breath kept flaming down her neck, gaining on her. Even Solly felt its relentless drain on his happy-go-lucky nature. That was why he always hollered at the children about leaving the doors open.

"Close that door, dummy! What you think I'm trying to do? Heat all of outdoors?"

In an effort to make her environment more predictable, Jewel began to perform little rituals to make her feel as if the universe had some order. Frequentation became her ally and her anchor.

"We have to say a prayer before we eat," she'd say at the dinner table. She made sure that they ate dinner together. She tried to make sure she kissed her children at night and made them say their prayers.

Most of the children said, "Jesus wept," when they went around the table with each child saying an individual blessing. But Solly could say a blessing over dinner— regardless of staying out at night—like none other. It was times like this, that Jewel called a truce in her heart and laid her sword down.

Jewel named the new baby, Paige Caldonia — the first name taken out of a white magazine, and the middle name after her mother-in-law — since Martha Grace had Luralee's middle name. Jewel found that the baby cried incessantly. The baby's face would screw up and her eyes would knit together in rebellion until it made Jewel's nerves just about stand up and tap dance on her skull. So much so that Jewel began to filch Solly's Pall Mall cigarettes to relax herself. Although she choked at first, the tobacco soothed her nerves. Since it was not ladylike to smoke openly in front of the children, or on the streets, Jewel hid in the bathroom. She felt guilty about smoking since she had been brought up to believe that smoking was the "devil's workshop," but she had to do something. Sometimes she wondered if the baby cried, because she knew Jewel had not wanted her. Instead of making the baby more humble, it seemed her unwelcome arrival had made her more stubborn and cranky, Jewel noticed.

After Paige's birth, Luralee came to stay with Jewel for two weeks. From the time Luralee opened the front door and crossed the threshold into the living room, Jewel could see the look of disgust and pity mirrored in Luralee's eyes. It reminded her of how she held her breath every time her mother's sister, Aunt Sunday, who also lived in Detroit, came to visit. That same condescending air that could choke Jewel. Whether they knew it or not, Jewel was a proud person. Their sniffs of disapproval did not go unnoticed. Although Jewel had cleaned the house from top to bottom, suddenly, she could see her house as it filtered through Luralee's eyes. For the first time, Jewel noticed the worn linoleum on the living room floor. Three fat brown roaches sauntered leisurely across the davenport, as if to say, "Look at me! Look at me!"

But worst of all, the ragamuffin-looking children of hers. It seemed as if all her boys' pant knees had been patched. When Solly was safely out of ear shot, Luralee said, "When you gonna learn, Jewel? You just like Mama."

"What do you mean? I was breast-feeding—"

Luralee didn't answer. The silence, as uncanny as a ringing tin pan, boomeranged through the room. Jewel tried to ignore her and went on with the unpacking.

She had just about forgotten Luralee's remark, when her mother started at it again.

"Why do you think Mama was so quiet when we were growing up?"

"I don't know what you mean," Jewel replied.

"She was so angry at Papa. Sometimes I think that's what sent her to bed before her time."

Jewel shifted the baby from one shoulder to the next, as she burped her.

"You know how Papa used to stay out as long as he pleased. It seemed like whenever he showed up, he was just there to drop off another baby for the older ones of us to help raise. At first, I think Mama used to really love Papa. But over the years—with him catting around and all—I think Mama started hating him."

Jewel was too stunned to speak. She had idolized Papa, even though she had known, through eavesdropping, about Miss Trudy, Papa's "Outside Woman."

"One time Papa even had the nerve to show up when some woman had cut him, expecting Mama to bandage his behind up."

"'Babe,' he had said, holding on to his arm, 'They cut me.'"

"What did Mama Lovey do?"

"Why she bandaged him up! I'll never forget it long as I live. I was the one who had to mop up all the blood. If Mama hadn't known how to make those poultices he probably would have bled to death."

"Why did she bandage him up? I wish Solly would pull that mess on me."

Jewel wished she had kept her mouth shut the instant the words fell out.

Thinking of Eldoretha Gray, she knew she was a hypocrite.

"She didn't have any choice," Luralee went on. "What could a woman who couldn't read do — what with eighteen babies?"

"Ummm-ummm-ummm."

"I watched Mama grow more and more bitter. 'Til she barely spoke at all. Especially after Miss Trudy sent her that cow's milk."

"What are you trying to say, Mama?"

"I'm just trying to say I don't want to see you wind up like Mama. Papa died old and satisfied. Mama died old and bitter."

Jewel didn't want Luralee to know how unhappy she was, so she turned away. She knew where Luralee was headed with the conversation. Jewel never talked to anyone about Solly.

"Aw Solly's all right, Mama."

"Is he back to work yet?" Luralee looked pointedly at Jewel.

"He may start doing some construction work. Just wait

'til you see that bar-b-que pit he built me in the back yard."

"Hmpph. Well, turn around and let me bind your stomach up. Hand me that towel and your pen cushion. Hope you have enough safety pens left."

The whole time Luralee penned the towel together, she fussed.

"Your stomach getting bigger after each baby. And look at your breast, so shriveled up, it's a shame. I know you can't be planning on nursing this baby. You getting so skinny your stomach make you look like a scare crow that done swallowed a watermelon."

"Mama, please."

"And look at that Solly — nigger just as young looking as new money."

"Now, Mama, I don't like you talking about my husband."

Jewel really thought Luralee had a lot of nerve. What did she know about keeping a husband? Already, she and Zach were sleeping in separate rooms. Just like Aunt Sunday and Uncle Jake. What did they know about love?

"All right," Luralee conceded. "I just don't like to see you looking all long-faceded, while that Peter Pan husband of yours looking as young as the day you married him."

Jewel could not answer, she was so angry. What gave Luralee the right to come in here, talking about her husband, when she did not even raise her? Was she worried about her looking long-faceded when she was a child, crying for her mother? Jewel didn't know how to speak up and put her hurt and abandonment into words.

"Hmmm. He just like that preacher father of his," Luralee went on. "Just because you way up North, don't think I don't know what's going on. Sunday be writing and telling me things. I know he ain't changed. A leopard

don't change its spots. Think I done forgot when y'all was
newlyweds down to his Mama's and him staying out half
the night no quicker than you spit Solly Junior out? I was
there when Solly Junior was born, and I know for a fact you
almost died. Think he cared though?

"Every month Illy and Sunday and I'm scraping up
quarters trying to make sure y'all eat up here. What do you
go and do? Go and get another little crumb-crushing
weasel."

At that moment Paige woke up and began to meow in
little kitten cries.

"Oooh, let me see the little thing. Hmmm. She is kinda
cute. Poor baby. World of trouble out there for a colored
child. 'Specially a girl child. You get yourself down to the
doctor and ask him to fit you with one of them diaphragm
things. I hear the young girls at work talking about them.
You hear me, Jewel Mae?"

THE WILDERNESS

After Paige's birth, Jewel sank into a depression so deep that Luralee had to come back that winter to help out. And it wasn't that Jewel asked for help, either. That was what was so frightening about the whole thing. Jewel didn't know she needed help, herself. Although Jewel was a prolific writer of letters, they all started out the same way.

Dear Mama,

How are you and everyone? Fine, I hope. Give everyone my love. We are fine.

But in her head sometimes, Jewel composed a letter to her relatives which went more like this:

Dear Kinfolk (or People)

I know you're my people because you're my mother's sisters. I'd like to leave Solly and come stay with you with my six kids. They don't eat a lot.

Jewel would laugh hysterically at the ludicrousness of it all. Who would ever take in a woman with six children? To think she'd thought her life would be better than Luralee's, and here her life was worse. She could still see the ghost of the young girl she was, who had laughed and told Luralee, "I'm going to have the best things in life. I'm not going to work all the time when I have children. I'm going to stay home with my children." Oh, the foolish, blind dreams of youth!

At the time that Jewel pronounced this vow, Luralee was working twelve-hour afternoon shifts. Jewel was too young to understand that even those long tours of duty were an improvement over what Luralee had endured as a live-in domestic with only one day off a week. Luralee no longer merely sent money to care for her children.

For the first time since they were babies, they lived with her on a day-to-day basis. Luralee's new husband, Zach, was polite, if distant, yet posed no problems. Jewel and Bubba saw Luralee every morning after she worked the afternoon shift. And if Luralee wasn't at home when they came in from school, they were always welcome to spend the evening at Aunt Mercy D's house. Still, Jewel had wanted more from Luralee, but it seemed as if her mother could never fill the void to make up for that loss of those first twelve years they were apart.

One day, as she had her hands up to her elbows in dish washing suds, Jewel paused. She pondered on how her words had come to haunt her. *Look at me,* her heart condemned her. Jewel didn't have the words in her head to express how disenchanted, disillusioned, and disemboweled her spirit felt. Her life seemed more like the slave life Papa used to describe than the happy life she'd imagined for herself as a young girl. She was overworked and underpaid. Yes, she stayed home with her children, but look at the price she paid for the journey. Her hands and feet were practically bare. Often she didn't have panties to put on her behind, or they had so many holes in them that she would get tired of sewing them up. Her life's condition was just too unspeakable for words. Whenever she looked into the mirror, she saw an empty hole. What had happened to the American Dream for the little brown girls all over the country? The little white house with the picket fence? The Knight in Shining Armor? The Happy-Ever-After ending?

One morning after the baby, Paige, had cried all night, her boys had fought all the previous day, and Solly had stayed out half the night, Jewel woke up with a tooth ache. She was more frustrated than she was in pain, when she put her head down on the kitchen table and had a good cry. She'd thought that all the children were outside playing, when suddenly, a small palm began to pat her in the square of her back. The hand patted her like a mother soothing a baby. Jewel looked up and saw Midge, teary-eyed herself.

"What's the matter, Mama?" The fear she saw in Midge's eyes mirrored her own. Wiping her eyes, Jewel said, "I'm all right. Just got something in my eyes." I must never let my children see me break like this, Jewel decided. If she was lost, how could she tell them anything? Who would they have, if she was falling apart?

No wonder she could hardly discipline her children. Because she had always felt so cheated out of a childhood, Jewel always overcompensated with her children. They sensed that she hated to whip them, so they were unruly. The least hardheaded out of the group were Joey and Judge, she decided. Midge and Cake Sandwich were just downright incorrigible. Her children jumped on the bunk beds until they stayed broken down and had to be replaced every year. The children leaned on the back of the kitchen chairs until the backs invariably broke off before the cheap furniture could even be paid for.

Because Jewel allowed her children to eat freely and without asking, the refrigerator door all but hung off the hinges. The deep freezer, which Jewel kept in the kitchen, almost didn't freeze because the children opened it so.

91

Sometimes, Jewel would think about setting restrictions on the food, but the ghost of her old childhood hunger cramps would come back to haunt her. She could still hear the sound of Aunt Beulah, on the other side of the bedroom wall, as she crunched nuts and candy under the cover.

Whenever this memory would surface, Jewel could actually feel her stomach grumble, even if she had gone to bed as full as a tic. No, she couldn't do that. She never wanted a child of hers to go through what she had gone through. So Jewel cooked sumptuous meals—fried chicken on Sundays, five-layered coconut cakes, mash potatoes, string beans, and corn on the cob.

When food was low, Jewel made "new dishes," which ingredients she would not divulge to her family, but which usually consisted of leftovers she called mulligan stew or minced meat pie. She also learned how to make bread pudding from leftover bread ends and raisins. That day, though, when her rice burnt, Jewel fell into a bottomless crying jag that she couldn't stop. She just couldn't seem to help herself. What had started out as a "little tiny weep" had turned into a tornado of tears. By then, all the children were standing around watching. The baby, Paige, woke up from a nap and began to wail. Midge, being a take-charge child and considering herself a big girl, got on the phone and called Aunt Sunday.

"Aunt Sunday. Something's wrong with Mama. She won't stop crying."

"Where's your Daddy?" Aunt Sunday asked.

"I dunno." The next thing Jewel knew, Luralee somehow managed to get time off of her job and come live with the Shepherds. Luralee's husband, Zach, came with her, too. While Jewel moved around like a zombie, Luralee washed her grandchildren's clothes in the tub, cooked simple meals, and tried to keep the older children quiet. Under Luralee's scorching gaze, Solly even came home early at night and tried to help.

"Nurse the baby," Luralee had to tell Jewel at appropriate intervals, because her dress bodice would be stained. Somehow, the baby thrived in this house of despondency. Whereas Paige's eyebrows used to knit together in discontentment at her unhappy entrance into the world, her eyes seemed to sparkle as she got older, and she cooed and gurgled like a singing brook. Following Paige's birth, and for a few years thereafter, Jewel blanked out blocks of time. Shadows moved. Sounds reverberated. Her thoughts were tattered, swinging doors in her mind—full of possibilities, but she was too afraid to go through them. The ground seemed to be sinking beneath her feet. A sense of malaise lingered and permeated every crook and cranny of her being. She no longer just felt like a fly trapped in a spider's web, she felt like her brain had become a maze with no outlet. Her thoughts spun around and around in her head like a broken record.

"I can't think too much," she decided. "I can't feel too much. I mustn't talk about it."

The reservoir of strength which Mama Lovey had imparted to her seemed to evaporate. The emotional disturbance formed shade patterns in the forest of her mind. She was in a rut and the wheels of life were crushing her. Her daily tasks became anchors in the present. Yesterday was a shadow. Tomorrow—she couldn't worry about it. She could only concern herself with getting through each moment. Like an alcoholic following a blackout, Paige's babyhood was lost to Jewel, swallowed up by a black hole of depression. When Jewel began to come back to herself, Paige was a little girl—almost three years old—a little girl who loved to rub her mother's legs encased in nylon hose. While Jewel talked on the phone, Paige curled around her lower legs like a tiny kitten, basking in her mother's warmth. Jewel's and Paige's earliest memories of each other were intricately intertwined with the telephone and nylon stockings.

"Ha'mercy." Jewel always murmured at appropriate intervals between lapses in the conversation on the telephone. Jewel was always a good listener, so there was never more than a dribble of conversation on her end.

"Hush your mouth."

"Sho'nuff?" Meantime, down on the floor, rubbing her mother's stockings, Paige thought her mother had a friend named "Shenna," she heard Jewel say "Sho'nuff," so much.

Slowly, Jewel began the long descent out of the abyss of despair. The thought of Solly's profligate waste of money on drink no longer threw her into a fit. The tenuous tightrope beneath her feet, which she was so afraid that just one wrong step on her part would plunge her into the precipices of madness, disappeared.

"I am going to save myself for something better," she told herself one day. Like many other mothers with small children, Jewel's vision was myopic. Just get through this moment. One foot after the other. One second at a time. One minute here. Now another hour. Then, all of a sudden, one day, Jewel looked up to see that Cake Sandwich and Judge were standing eyeball to eyeball with her. In the outside world, a new president had come and gone. One other good thing had come out of those dark years. While Paige was a baby, Jewel, taking Luralee's advice, had gone to Doctor Baker and was fitted with a diaphragm. She wore it faithfully every night from that point forward. Jewel still loved Solly, but she couldn't see

94

herself having any more of his babies. She could no longer stand how dead each baby made her feel. As if her heart had turned to stone. As if she had lost the capacity to feel anything. And that was worse than being dead.

Summer was usually a good time for Jewel. The laundry, drying on the lines in the back yard, held the memory of the lakes surrounding Michigan. Jewel buried her nose in the threads of the sheets when she gathered them off the line and reveled in the eternity found in their scents. For her, summer was filled with other wonderful perfumes. Roses. Lilacs. Tiger lilies. Hyacinths. Cherry blossoms. African violets. And sounds. Every wonderful lark, robin, and sparrow raised its voice in melodic symphony for her.

Best of all, the children could go out and play. In the winter, the children acted as moldy and mildewed as the laundry she would hang in the dank, damp basement. But in the summer, they blossomed, competing with the flowers in their rejuvenation.

The summer Paige was born went by in a blur, but the baby's second summer was a little better. Luralee had stayed from December to June, and Jewel was both glad and relieved to see her go. Although she still felt weak, she felt that she could handle everything now — by herself. Luralee had been so bossy that Jewel finally understood what people meant when they said there could only be one woman in a household.

One day, Jewel put her two toddling babies in the yard with her, as she hung up her clothes. So far that summer, Baby Boy had pulled a hot iron down on his head while she was trying to heat one of Paige's bottles. But the hot iron had only glanced his face, and the color was coming back already. All in all, when Jewel watched swatches of azure sky play hide and seek with the clouds, she knew she just had to hold on. Things were going to be better tomorrow.

Solly seemed pleased enough with the new baby. That summer he even went to church one Sunday with Jewel and all six children.

"Doesn't matter if he has one or ten babies. His freedom goes on and on," Jewel thought sullenly to herself.

That particular Sunday, perhaps in seeing Solly as one of the lost sheep from the flock, Pastor Patton seemed more lit up with brimstone and hellfire than usual.

"Remember the Lord in some of his ways is mysterious. The Bible say so. There is some born under the power of the Lord for to do good and overcome the evil power. Now, you see good people, that produces two forces, like fire and water. The evil forces starts the fire and I has the water force to put it out."

"Yes, Lord," Old Deacon Shaw enjoined.

"Preach," added Elder Berry.

"Let not sin," the Reverend, in menacing clouds, intoned, "I say, let not sin—"

"Amen."

"Reign—"

"Yes, Lord."

"In your body."

"Tell it now."

"Cause sin—"

"Go on now—"

"Only has a season."

Jewel looked over at Solly, hoping he was listening. Instead, Solly was dozing, spit dribbling out of the corners of his mouth, head nodded to his chest. . . .

Before Jewel could try to nudge Solly awake, Miss Lenore sang Jewel's favorite solo, and Jewel envisioned herself in heaven, she felt so transported on the chariot of melancholic notes.

Precious Lord, take my hand...

At the end of the song, Miss Helen started to get "happy" with the "Holy Ghost." Racing up the aisles, arms outstretched, she was a bird in flight, shouting to the stranger whom she wanted to deliver her. The female ushers had to call three men to help hold her down, while she fought like a cornered tigress. Miss Helen was at least eighty-five years old, but it seemed to Jewel, she got feistier each year. There was a sorrow, as mournful as a blood-red moon, yet a joy as ancient as the rivers, etching the echoes of her screams.

Jewel looked over at the end of the pew and saw that Miss Helen's screams had awakened Solly. Cake Sandwich, Midge, and Judge were covering their mouths, to keep the snickers from bursting through their fingers. The baby woke up and began to cry. Jewel was surprised when Solly took the baby and walked Paige outside, giving her an unaccustomed break.

Solly wasn't all bad, Jewel mused. One thing she admired about Solly, was how he reigned as the thane of thunder, liege of lightning in his house. Since Solly was not only the stronger, but the more consistent disciplinarian of the two, Jewel always warned Cake Sandwich and Judge, "Wait 'til your father gets home. He is going to get you."

And whip, he would. Jewel usually ended up stopping him.

"You're killing my child. Stop! Stop!"

Jewel also marveled at how everyone—including herself—waited on Solly. Jewel picked his bumps and shaved him every Saturday night. Solly sat in a kitchen chair, and Jewel, with an apron wrapped around her waist, worked from a bowl of water, as she stood between his legs.

Once Solly started doing construction work, the boys each took a foot and unlaced the hundred shoestring laces coated with mud that traveled up his brogan boots. He had also taken all four boys, one by one, to work with him, but none were interested in bricklaying.

Sometimes, Jewel envied Solly his "joie-de-vivre." He was the gregarious one of the two, and men friends flocked to the back door. Without exception, Jewel hated all of his friends—almost as much as she hated it if she didn't see them come over and had no idea where Solly was. It was generally Solly who offered a stranger a meal, whereas Jewel, who counted every bite she had to scrape up for her own children, foamed at the mouth. She could not fathom the idea of how Solly took to stray men.

But Solly would come back and tell Jewel stories that he and his men friends told—"Tall Tales"—which she loved to hear. Her favorite story was the one that Solly told her about how their friend, John Henry Jackson, left the South.

John Henry Jackson was a sharecropper in Natchez, Mississippi before he came North to Delray. One Monday morning, after carousing all weekend, he went to work with a hangover.

John Henry's job was to lead the mule out of the barn and into the fields. This particular day, the mule wouldn't budge. When John Henry commenced to cursing him, the mule hauled off and kicked him. Before John Henry knew it, he had pulled out his knife and cut the mule. Now, the overseer happened to be outside the barn and saw what John Henry did.

The overseer, a white man, felt more human feeling for a mule than for any two-legged being called "a nigger," so he came inside of the barn and threw John Henry out into the yard.

In a split second, the overseer got on top of John Henry and was getting the best of him. John Henry said he didn't know what made him pull back out his knife on a white man in the South, but he must have been possessed.

Whatever the case, he commenced to goosing the overseer with his knife. By the time the overseer staggered off John Henry, his shirt was splattered with as much blood as a chicken running around after its head had been cut off. John Henry ran all the way to his cabin on the sharecropping rows.

Once he reached there, his wife, Frannie, who'd been looking out of the window, had a little sack packed with his things. They didn't have to say a word. They both knew that either the man's brothers or the Klu Klux Klan would be coming for John Henry before the sun went down.

John Henry said he set out running through the swamps so fast that he cried out, "Lord, you just move those big trees and I'll take care of the sapling bushes!"

And he didn't stop running until he made it to Delray, Michigan.

Solly always ended the story with, "That John Henry know he can lie." Jewel loved to hear a story when Solly told it.

       *   *   *   *   *   *   *   *   *

Because Jewel was determined to have the family life she'd felt she'd been deprived of as a child, in times of truce in her marriage, she affectionately called Solly, "Daddy Laddy." Sometimes, she called him "Daddy Sweet." Solly, in turn, called Jewel, "Momooskey."

When she was a child, Jewel had never had a nickname. This was another slight she'd felt she'd suffered. When she had lived with her cousins, she noticed how Aunt Beulah and Uncle Thed had nicknames for all of their children. Walline was "Butter Cup." Zenola was "Baby Cakes."

Thed Junior was "Son." Little Joshua—Jewel's special favorite—was "Scooter." Jewel couldn't help but feel left out. A nickname was that something special parents reserved for their child. Because she didn't have her mother or father with her there was always that something special missing. That indefinable quality she would watch that went on between Beulah and her kids.

"Bring your crazy butt out of the rain," had a different quality to it when Beulah addressed her own kids, than when she called Jewel and Bubba.

And now that Jewel had her own children, she finally understood what it was. It was like watching the carmine rim of a sunset and knowing that it was all yours—good or bad. They belonged to you. And you would hold their hands all the way to an electric chair if you had to, because they represented you in the world.

Jewel saw her life like that of a tree. Her roots had been stunted in childhood, uplifted, and bruised. But in her adult life, her children were her branches out into the world. In their budding and flowering, she had a chance to touch the heavens.

That was why she gave her children pet nicknames. Solly Junior became "Cake Sandwich," because he liked his sandwiches layered with three slices of bread.

Joseph was "Joey." Midge was "Sissy" after Luralee, whose nickname was "Sister." Gideon was called "Judge," because of his sober nature.

From the time he was old enough to open his eyes, Judge had always kept one eye squinted from an accident suffered at his birth, a rather botched home delivery in the South. Luralee, in an attempt to aid the midwife, tried to squeeze the drops of silver nitrate into his eyes, but she was so nervous, that she missed one eye. Thereafter, the neighborhood children called Judge "Sleepy" after the "Seven Dwarfs." Naturally, Paige became "Baby." Only "Baby Boy," as she called her youngest son, Daniel, seemed to resent his nickname.

At dinner time, when Jewel stood on her front porch, one by one, calling her children in her mellifluous voice, she found that Daniel was the only one who refused to answer to "Baby Boy."

He always said, "Aw, Ma. Don't be embarrassing me in front of my friends. And I don't want you kissing on me, either."

Had Solly been born of a different hue, perhaps even in a different time, his life might have turned out differently. Later, when he was older, Solly would always remember a poem that he learned at Booker T. Washington High School. It had been written more than a century ago by John Greenleaf Whittier.

For all sad words of tongue or pen,
The saddest are these 'It might have been!'

When Solly was a boy, the American Dream was an exclusive club with an invisible sign claiming "For White Boys Only." He knew of the rags-to-riches story of Horatio Alger. He knew of the Abe Lincoln story, and his rise from logsplitting to directing the office of the United States' Presidency. However, he knew, even as a young boy, that he could never grow up to be President. In fact, he was told he would be lucky if he grew up at all as a black male in the South. Like unformed clay, Solly was still too malleable, too much a product of his times, to challenge the world. It seemed as though all of his Southern upbringing had defeated him before he had developed enough to challenge Jim Crow. One day his high school teacher, Mr. Winfield, told him, "Do like Booker T. Washington, our great Founder, said. Work with your hands, Solomon. Don't be listening to this troublemaker W.E.B. Du Bois."

Later, at Mountain View University, his English professor, Doctor Brooks, told him, "Solomon, I notice you are a natural-born storyteller. Have you ever thought of becoming a writer?"

Solly knew he could captivate audiences with his Thespian talents at the pool room and the barber shop with his telling of a story, but he had never known anyone colored to make a living as a writer. Maybe Langston Hughes. And hadn't Paul Lawrence Dunbar drank himself to death? Most of the black men Solly knew were porters, dish washers, elevator operators, and tradesmen. Even his learned professors had to moonlight in menial jobs in order to be able to support their families.

"No, I think I'll be going into the trades," Solly said. "You never heard too much about a colored writer making a living, have you?"

Professor Brooks said something that Solly thought was strange. "What if Frederick Douglas had had that attitude, and here he was, born a slave? Solomon, sometimes we have invisible chains that we put on our brains, and they don't have anything to do with slavery." Solomon Shepherd had graduated at the top of his class. In his senior yearbook he said that he aspired to be rich. When the day finally came for his ship to come in, a shipwreck blew his dreams away. And without his dreams, he became a man without an anchor. Anchorless, he became bitter. And bitter, he became negative.

"You can't do that," he'd say.

"Yes, you can," Jewel would contradict him. "Don't discourage him, Daddy."

"Dummy."

"Knucklehead." But he hadn't started out that way. At one time, he had been voted "The Most Likely to Succeed." As a teenager, he had been likable and apt. His teachers at Booker T. Washington High had told him he could go to college. When he and Jewel got married, he dropped out of college. Although he never came out and put it in words, inside — in his naked, unadorned heart — he felt that if Jewel didn't have so many babies, he might be able to make it in the world. By the time Solly was drafted into World War II, Jewel had three babies.

Solly was stationed in Fort Lewis, Washington, where he got to see racism in its full whoredom dress. The colored troops were being used to dig the trenches over in wartorn Europe. He was never sent overseas because he had a wife and three children by the time the cauldron of war had started brewing. Jewel moved from Tulsa to Richmond, California to live near Solly's people. But she never liked California. Three years after Solly got out of the service, Jewel talked Solly into moving to Michigan where her cousins, Zenola and Thed Junior, had settled. Also, her mother's sister, Aunt Sunday, was living in Detroit with her husband, Uncle Jake, and said that they could live with them until they found a place to stay. Solly never knew the other reason Jewel wanted to get away from Richmond, California was that his in-laws helped Solly stay into too much devilment.

Solly graduated from the world of Uncle SAM, where he realized he was a pawn, to rulership over the vassals called his children. If he couldn't be lord out in the world, he made sure he was going to reign in his roost. The only sad thing about the whole matter was that Solly really loved his children. When he watched men — frustrated from not being able to sufficiently support their families without the wife taking on a little "days work" — walk off and leave their children day after day, he never left. But he still believed in sparing the rod, you spoiled the child. And no one had ever given him an outward display of love, so he never lavished any of the children in affection.

This attitude he inherited from his father, Judd Shepherd. Judd Shepherd had been a minister. It seemed to Solly, that his entire childhood had been spent in church or at a revival. His father had been called one of "The Never-Dies," so Solly shrank inside every time he had to go evangelizing with his father. He had sworn inside—as he put, "on a stack of Bibles"—that if he "ever got grown," he would never step foot in a church again. True to his boyhood vow, Solly became a stranger to the church's doorway. Only with Jewel's prodding and cajoling, did he make it several times the entire time that his family was growing up.

A satyr and a libertine from young manhood, it didn't take much for Solly to be derailed from his deepest dreams and desires. Women were always hanging like bats from the rafters of his choosing. The conventions of marriage did not preclude his partaking in the earthly delectable delights he saw everywhere he went. Solly, with his dark ebony skin, was a handsome muscular Black man. As a young man, he had a panther-like quality about him which women found very attractive. He also inherited another trait from his father—womanizing. But, unlike his father, Solly wasn't a hypocrite. He didn't choose the church to cloak his sins.

Because of Solly's understanding that America did not afford him the same privileges as manhood entitled white Homo Sapien males, Solly acted out his rites of passage in the arena of wine, women, and song. He never discussed how angry it made him feel when the Negro troops were good enough to dig latrines for the fighting white troops, but not good enough to fight side by side with the white soldiers. He never discussed how he felt when he couldn't get the same job as the young white men who could and would apply for an office job. Solly laughed a lot. He talked. A lot. But he seldom revealed the true Solly — even in his most intimate moments with Jewel. He had also learned that from his father, Judd Shepherd. When he was a boy, his father had beaten him with a hickory cane until he almost passed out.

"I'll kill you if you cry," he told him. It had been Solly's turn to help churn the butter. Solly and his little brother, A.J., had gotten into a fight and spilled the butter. "Go take off all your clothes," Judd had told Solly. His father had taken Solly back behind the wood pile shed and beat him with all the strength a former slave master would have beaten his ancestors. Solly had black marks along his middle and back, but Solly never cried. From that point on, Solly learned to hold his tears inside of a strongbox he kept under lock and key.

Whenever Solly chastised his children, he reiterated and reechoed many of Judd Shepherd's litanies.

"I'm gonna have to go crazy on you boy (gal). I been being too easy on you. Hard head make a sore behind. Don't listen to what I tell you, huh?"

As he would get wound up, sweat popping from his forehead, ironing cord wrapped around his large fists, he would beat even harder.

"You're a black nigger, you hear. No matter how far you go in life, you'll always be one. Tough titty." Sometimes when Solly had whipped the offending child or two in rhythmical lashes — accompanied by the cacophony of Jewel's cries — "Stop! You'll kill him!" — Solly reiterated the same messages. "I'll kill you little Nigger! Stole a car! Huh! Got drunk! Huh! You're a black nigger. And out there in that world, that's what you'll always be. I'll beat you, before the police kill you." If the offending child was bad enough, like the time Cake Sandwich stole a car, Jewel joined in on the beating, she was so afraid of ending up the mother of a jailbird.

Even when Solly wasn't chastising the children, he was intimidating. Solly could often be heard bellowing for one of the children through the screen door.

"Cake Sandwich! Judge! Midge!"

Whenever one of the children showed up, Solly ordered, "Get me a glass of water," or "Light me a cigarette on the stove."

"But Daddy, I was outside playing."

"That's what I had you for," Solly generally responded. Once they got the phone installed, Solly would call whoever was in the house to come answer it, since he was a people person, not a phone person.

"Daddy, how come I have to answer the phone and you're sitting right by it? I had just hit a home run in the alley when you called me."

"That's what I had you for."

When black and white television came out, there were only two channels. Whether it was a western or a game show, Solly chose whatever channel the family watched. Everyone gathered around his feet and contented themselves to watch whatever show Solly changed the channel to. No one questioned that it should be any other way. After all, Solly was the man of the house.

The first absinthe of negativism started to take root and grow when Solly was in the service. Later, the seed grew from a mustard grain to a weed, after Solly found that he could never be content to work for someone. He held down jobs as a bus driver, cook, welder, and finally, as a construction worker, which afforded him some outside freedom.

One spring, after finding out he and A.J. couldn't get into the teamster union, Solly came up with the idea that they should start their own little construction business. After about four months, when they couldn't get any contractors to do business with them as a small colored company in the early fifties, they had to close up shop. From that point on, Solly gave up hope of ever having his own business. Although he was freed in body, his spirit was still as shackled as his enslaved grandparents' had been.

One of his running litanies was always, "Niggers can't do this. Niggers can't do that. They won't let niggers do that."

1954

Jewel was going out that New Year's Eve for the first time in almost thirteen years of married life. She didn't care what Solly said. He was taking her to the teamsters' ball. Jewel felt that this dance was a step above the usual honky-tonk party that Solly frequented. Probably was out there doing the "booty-green," Jewel thought. Well, this dance sounded as if it was going to be of a higher-class and caliber. If and when she did get out, Jewel wanted to go somewhere nice.

The invitation had said "Formal Attire." Jewel still knew how to sew, and she rushed and pulled out a pattern. She had one Sunday dress to her name and a few house dresses. She wanted to have a new dress for this occasion.

A.J. and Cleotha, her sister-in-law, were going. Solly and Jewel were going to ride with the couple in their new Pontiac. Cleotha was going to buy her dress from Crowley's, but Jewel refused to let that dim her joy.

"Who's going to keep the brats?" Solly inquired. Jewel could read her husband's thoughts as they promenaded from the laboratory of his brain and issued out of his mouth. She finally had lived with Solly long enough to start out-thinking him.

"Rachel is coming over to keep the kids. Besides, Solly Junior and them are almost teenagers now. They can watch themselves."

Geneva was one of the newlyweds who, along with

her groom, rented a room in the upstairs. Rachel was her sixteen-year-old sister who lived down the street.

"How about the baby?"

"The baby is riding a tricycle—in case you hadn't noticed—and giving me a hard time keeping up with her to boot. I need a change. Wear your black suit, Solly. I guess it'll have to do."

Jewel was so excited to be going to a dance that she felt as carefree and frivolous as a girl again. This was the best she had felt in years. For the first time in over twelve years, she'd gotten a baby up to three-and-a-half and wasn't pregnant with another one. She was even beginning to string two thoughts together and see them stay connected.

Yes, for the first time since high school, she was making plans. Her first plan was to figure out how to get her family out of Delray. But tonight, she was not going to concern herself with her old enemy, worry. She was only going to pretend she was Cinderella going to the ball.

Jewel soaked her face in Vaseline. She washed her hair in rain water, then put a hard press on it. Jewel used the hard crimping clips to make waves on the sides of her head, and she tore up paper bags to curl the ends of her hair into a page boy. Jewel always kept her hair neat, but she took extra pains to make sure it looked especially nice for the dance. It reminded her of how excited she was when she and Solly used to go out on dates in high school. With the sewing machine that Luralee had sent her, Jewel copied a simple dirndl dress with a black velvet bodice.

The night of the dance, Jewel sprinkled herself with rose water. Luralee had sent her a fake fur wrap for Christmas, and she couldn't wait to wear it out.

As Jewel brushed rouge into her cheeks and sprinkled powder on her face, Midge looked on in the

111

mirror. Midge's eyes followed the trace of red lipstick which Jewel applied to her lips. Midge thought that her mother was the most beautiful woman in the world.

"Mama, you look so pretty." Midge's voice was lined with a sad wistfulness.

"You're pretty, too, baby," Jewel said, patting her head. Jewel felt the edges of sadness creeping into the corners of her smile. How come Midge's hair wouldn't grow anymore? She wished she had never cut off all of the child's hair when Midge had had ringworm when she was two years old. Jewel thought of the two fat braids Midge had had before she had cut her hair off. Midge's hair was of a coarser grade than Jewel's, and she could not do a thing with the child's hair. Matters were made worse by Midge's hair remaining so short.

"What you doing with all that Indian Paint on?" Solly said, coming into the bedroom, but Jewel could tell he was pleased.

Jewel, wearing a girdle she'd found at the goodwill, looked as slim as the one hundred-and-thirty-five pounds she actually weighed. Because her stomach perpetually sagged and protruded from the vestiges of her pregnancies, Jewel often had the appearance of a heavier woman. But dressed up and without a look of worry tugging at the corner of her eyes and mouth, Jewel resembled the singer and actress, Lena Horne.

Jewel made a promise to herself that night. She decided fervently that she was not gong to worry. Yes, she was going to put old man worry on the back burner.

That night she was not going to worry about the tenants, either. She refused to think about her roomer, Ronny Gunn, a single man, whom she was going to have to put out, because he was drinking too much. Solly didn't need any extra help or any new drinking buddies.

Yessireee. She was not going to fret that A.J. had gotten on at Chrysler two years ago and was now going to make foreman. She'd just be glad for them. And she'd be grateful that Solly had worked from May to December with a good construction team. The money had been good. She had been able to squirrel some away for winter. Yes, tonight was going to be her night. This was the beginning of the best year she'd had in a long time. She was beginning to dare hope again. Yes, tomorrow was a new day. Tomorrow would be better.

When they entered the local teamster's club house, on the northwest side of town, which was predominantly inhabited by whites, Jewel gasped. The room was dark, and the only light emanated from a spinning glass ball. Ferns decorated false columns painted white and gold. Plastic crawling ivy and arbor grapevines trailed down the columns.

Festoons of fake nasturtiums, marigolds, roses, and orchids decorated the tables. Each round table was covered with a white table cloth that gleamed in the dark, a candelabra sat in the center of each table and each could seat about ten people.

The local teamster's president and the other official members sat at a long rectangular table on a dais. A podium was centered in the middle of the table, for the master of ceremonies to usher in the New Year. Although there were white and colored at the dance, Jewel noticed the whites all sat near the front.

She didn't care, though. Jewel was so happy, bubbly

and excited, she couldn't help from "gushing."

Solly always complained about how effusive Jewel was. She loved to make over nice things. It drove him into frenzies as she described every minute detail without ever getting to the point whenever she related a story. Jewel had a tendency to travel over the ocean bed of the story before she ever reached the ship. She could be delivered to rapture over the sight of a flower opening. Jewel was one of those people for whom the journey was always an adventure, because she could soak and drench herself into the moment of the experience.

To Solly, Jewel was too excitable and giddy. But that night, Solly didn't complain too much about Jewel's ramblings. Jewel could tell that Solly was proud to have her on his arm.

After they were seated, Solly asked Jewel, "What do you want, Honey?"

"You can bring me a coke, Daddy," she said. "Don't get drunk," Jewel whispered as an afterthought, when Solly was walking towards the bar.

Solly threw her back a glare of defiance.

"You don't tell me what to do. I'm grown. Last I heard, my Mama was in Berkeley, California."

Jewel was so embarrassed, she just looked down at her hands. She had soaked her hands in Vaseline the night before and slept in gloves. Jewel's hands felt soft as the bottoms of her babies' feet before they started walking. They didn't look as if they stayed in water and bleach all the time.

Suddenly, Jewel noticed that she was sitting by herself. Cleotha and A.J. were already on the dance floor, dancing cheek to cheek. Sometimes, Jewel wished she and Solly got along as well as his brother, A.J., and his wife, got along. Now, that was one young couple who seemed to like the same things. When the couple had first moved to Detroit, they had lived with the Shepherds for six months. Jewel knew from living with A.J. and Cleotha that they were not putting up a front. They truly enjoyed one another's company. They both liked to dance, play Bid Whist, and drink a little highball once in a while.

Once, when they came over on Memorial Holiday, Jewel had tried to drink a beer, so that she could seem more sociable. The next thing she knew, the room was swirling, and she was lying in the bed with her head swimming in circles. She was so sick, she couldn't play her hand of Bid Whist. She had thrown up her ribs and her potato salad. Jewel had never been so sick. She never tried to drink again.

She couldn't glean what anyone saw in alcohol. But Solly seemed as if he just loved to drink. He didn't drink at all through the week, but he seemed to get his hands on liquor on most weekends. Once he got the hot liquid down in his chest, Solly lit up like firecrackers on The Fourth of July. That was when, with the liquor loosening up his tongue, that Solly opened up and told Jewel stories.

Sometimes, although Jewel would never admit it, she found Solly to be more fun when he was drinking than when he was sober.

The teamsters had hired a colored band. Although they made a halfhearted effort to play renditions of jazz greats such as Miles Davis, Charlie Parker, and John Coltrane, they finally found their pitch and broke into a fury of funky, lowdown dirty blues. The whole hall came alive as people bumped and grinded to the tunes of B.B. King, Muddy Waters, and Billie Holiday.

*   *   *   *   *

"Hit me, but don't quit me!"

Jewel was let down by seeing "The Funk" take over, yet she couldn't help but notice how lively the place had become since the blues, like a loose-living woman crashing a prayer meeting, had come out of hiding.

Sitting alone and watching the crowd sway from side to side, she recalled what had attracted her to Solly in the first place. Oh, could Solly dance! He thought she didn't see him over on the other side of the room.

Jewel started to get up and go knock him upside his head. He was dancing away with a woman whose hair was too blond to be true. The woman was dark-skinned. Jewel wondered if she was wearing a wig. Didn't she know her tone of skin color didn't go with a white woman's wig?

Jewel wondered if Solly liked dark-skinned women. She had never given his color a thought. It had been his legs which first attracted Jewel to Solly. Solly was sitting in the barber's chair at the local barber shop in Tulsa, when she first went to live with Luralee. From the way his mouth was moving up and down, he was telling a story. The men were laughing all around him. Jewel, who pretended to be walking to the ice cream parlor with her girl friend, Alice, couldn't help but observe how he had his pant legs pulled up to his knees. His legs were hard and muscular. The veins stood out like ropes on a ship, they were so big.

Jewel knew from that very moment, she wanted to get to know this boy whom she'd seen dropping their newspaper off on their front porch.

Jewel's reverie was interrupted by a man's voice.

"May I have this dance?"

Jewel was startled to see a nice-looking, apricot-colored man standing before her with his hand outstretched.

"That's all right. I don't dance."

The man lingered on and made conversation.

"A nice-looking woman like you, don't dance? Well, it's easy. You can do the two step."

Jewel weighed her options. A.J. and Cleotha were glistening with sweat and laughter over in the middle of the dance floor. She hadn't seen Solly's head in the crowd for some time. In fact, so many people were out on the floor maybe no one would notice if she made a faux pas—a word she'd seen in a magazine—or if she stepped on the man's feet.

"Sure," Jewel replied, trying to sound airy and vivacious.

Jewel, never a good dancer to begin with, had not danced in so many years she didn't know what to do. Although she was a little awkward at first, the man was a good dancer, and slowly, Jewel fell into step with him.

"Nice dance," the man was saying softly.

"Yes," Jewel answered, being sure not to show the cavity which had began to dominate her front teeth. She wondered why she even cared.

Suddenly, she felt someone tapping her on her shoulder. Jewel turned around, surprised to see Solly standing beside the dancing couple.

Jewel could tell by the whites of his eyes that Solly was angry. Jealous, too.

"May I cut in on this dance?" Solly asked the man.

The man, whose name Jewel never learned, stepped away with an amused grin on his face. He took a deep bow directed at Jewel and tipped his head to Solly.

The rest of the night, Solly never left Jewel's side.

PAIGE

Winter 1956

Gazing at the snowflakes falling outside the window pane, Paige knew the loneliness of time. At five years of age, she only went to kindergarten for half-a-day, whereas all of her older brothers and her sister were gone to school all day. She missed her brother, Danny, because he had been her main playmate before he started school all day.

She wanted to go out and make mudpies or play in the sandbox Daddy had built for her, but the snow covered up everything. Snow weighed down the bare limbs of the mulberry tree in the back yard. It bent the boughs of the maples, oaks, and elms lining Cottrow Street.

Paige wanted Mama to leave an empty bowl on the back porch so that she could make that magical substance she called "ice cream." Mama knew how to mix the snow with vanilla and sugar. Mama was just about the best Mama in the whole wide world.

When Paige went out on the back porch to break off an icicle from the eaves where the back porch slanted, Mama said, "No, Baby. That's dirty. You'll get germs."

Paige liked to suck icicles. Mama was the meanest Mama in the whole wide world.

Next, Mama wouldn't let her go out and make angels in the snow.

"You just got over the mumps, Baby. You can't go out there. You might get sick."

"Can I go play over at Smokey's?"

Smokey, Paige's little girlfriend, was the first playmate she ever had. She lived across the street from them. Miss Lenore was her mother.

"You know you got hit by a car last summer, and I don't want nothing bad to happen to my Baby."

"Why come?"

"Because that's how Mamas feel about their baby girls."

"Can I go over to Rosemary's?"

"No. You know your Daddy said you better not go back down there. Remember when the police brought you home in their car? We thought something bad had happened to our little girl when you didn't come home from school."

"Aw shoot. Mama, I want somebody to play with."

Paige folded her arms and pouted. Why did Mama think the world was such a dangerous place? She had only stopped to play at a new girl's house after kindergarten let out in the morning. After she ate rice, chicken, and gravy for dinner, she was walking down the street when the white policeman picked her up and put her in the big black police car. As soon as she made it to the back door, she saw Daddy standing in the hallway with the belt twisted around his wrist ready to whip her. How come he had put the belt behind his back when he saw the police?

"Thank you for bringing her home, sir," Daddy had said to the police.

Shoot. Paige wanted to have fun. But the world was still an ocean bed of discovery, so she sat and looked around the living room. The living room's clock said "Coo-coo" at some indeterminate interval that Paige hadn't figured out yet. The picture of the white baby on the bedroom wall made her think of the angels that Mama said had brought her to this family. Sometimes, Mama said a stork delivered babies. Now which one was it?

So, sometimes Paige dreamed about the white angels or the white stork bringing her and dropping her down the chimney like white Santa Claus did. Anyway, how did Santa Claus get his fat self down that little pipe they had on their roof?

The flowers from the wall paper were green, yet she could see the old red wall paper which was underneath the latest layer. Paige often hid behind the brown sofa from the ghouls of her nightmare, "The Boogey Man" and the old tramp everyone called "Hobo Joe." This was also a fortress wall when she and Danny played Cowboys and Indians. Behind the safe harbor of the sofa, Paige hid from her big brother, Danny, as he raced around on a broomstick which doubled as his "horsie" whenever they played Cowboys and Indians. Danny always had to be "The Cowboy." Paige was assigned the role of "The Indian." Sometimes they played "Tarzan and the Savages" or "The Africans." Then, Paige had to play "The Africans."

Danny said Africans were black. Paige knew that she was colored. Danny had said so. The Black Africans were bad. Colored was bad, too. Or why wouldn't they have more colored people on besides Amos and Andy?

Every since Paige had been hit by a car, Jewel wouldn't let her go out as much. Paige knew it had happened sometime in the summer before she started school. That day was still a potato-hole in the sock of her memory. She could only remember the hot glass on the sidewalk. She and a little girl named Faye were playing a game of "Dare you to push me into the street." They were standing at the curb. Paige couldn't believe it when Faye actually pushed her under the fast approaching car. She never remembered the car hitting her. She only remembered squeezing her eyes real tight, then opening them again. She had been amazed at the labyrinth of pipes up under the car when she opened her eyes. She could still taste the gas in her throat. The next thing she remembered Mama was driving her to the hospital and bringing her back that night. What did Mama mean by she could've been killed? She was only playing a game.

So, Paige was happy when finally, the monotony of the day was broken up when her girlfriend, Smokey, came over to play.

"Come on in, Emma Jean," Mama said, face broken into a waterfall of smiles.

She liked Smokey, but she didn't like any of the other little girls that Paige tried to bring home.

Mama always asked, "Well, whose child are you?" as she examined them as one would examine a patient for lice. "Who are your people? Where does your family live?"

"What do you want to play?" Smokey asked, as soon as she got into Jewel's bedroom.

"Let's make like we're white," Paige said.

The two little girls knew the ritual well. They both went into Jewel's drawers where she kept her scarves. They each wrapped a brightly-colored scarf around their heads, letting the tails trail down their backs. This was a regular game they played, along with Little Sally Walker, freeze, or hopscotch.

"I'ma be Shirley Temple," Smokey said. Looking at herself in the mirror, her wiry upturned braids framed a round face which beamed with Goldilocks-dream expectations. Standing next to her, Paige stared at her own reflection. She was the sponge color of the mulberries in the backyard — the color they had in the spring just before they became ripe. Smokey was the color of full-blown summer mulberries — indigo plum.

But the two girls, staring in the mirror, didn't see their color. They pictured what they saw reflected in books and on television. White. Now, they'd have the same adoring smiles cast upon them. The same adulation.

"No, let's play Snow White. I'ma be Snow White. You be the Wicked Queen."

"You always have to be it," Smokey grumbled, but went along with Paige's suggestions. Smokey was only four, and she idolized Paige.

"It" was generally the "Mama" when they played house, the "leader" when they played tag, or the "hider" when they played hide and seek.

Paige knew most of the plots to fairy tales because Mama read to her all the time.

Even so, Smokey complied. "Oh, Mirror, Mirror on the wall. Who's the fairest of them all?"

"I am. I am," cried Paige.

"No, you're not. Snow White is the fairest in the land."

"Well, silly, I'm Snow White. You so dumb. I told you I was Snow White, girl."

"Well, I'm going to kill you."

The game ended with The Wicked Queen chasing Snow White all over the bedroom.

"Baby, stop running all over the place," Jewel called out from the kitchen.

A knock came at the door. It was the little white boy, Chris, from next door. Mrs. Slovik was his mother, and Mama liked her better than most of her neighbors.

"Come on in, Chris."

Usually, when there was more than one child visiting, Jewel threw her hands in the air and started reciting her litany.

"I told you I can't stand droves of kids coming over here, Baby. If it's not you with somebody, it's Midge with Buckeye or Cake Sandwich with Pee Wee. Ooh Brother! Heavenly Father!"

"I know y'all better not be playing nasty in there," Jewel warned today.

"We ain't."

Jewel didn't realize this was the game that Paige and Smokey entered into only with her two little black boyfriends, Robert Earl and Boot. The children would try to figure out each other's anatomy through looking and rubbing.

With Chris joining the group, the girls could now play "The Three Bears" or "Little Red Riding Hood." Chris always played the Big Bad Wolf. Just as the Big Bad Wolf was about to jump out of the bed and eat Little Red Riding Hood, a loud voice bellowed at the front door.

"Is the Mom-mooskey home?" It was Daddy.

"I'm in here, Daddy Laddy," Mama called from the kitchen. Daddy was just getting in from work. He was caked in snow and mud and looked like a giant brown snowman.

Smokey and Chris looked at each other and burst out laughing. Paige had never thought anything was unusual about her family before this time.

The rest of the afternoon was spent playing variations of "Is the Mom-Mommoskey home?" One form of the new game involved Christmas.

Chris, pretending to be Santa Claus in the North Pole, rang up the house on the imaginary play phone.

Smokey answered, "Hello."

"May I speak to the Momooskey of the house?" Santa Claus asked.

Going to school was another new world for Paige. She learned to stand in line and raise her hand when she wanted her turn to speak. She also learned that the children with the pink skin got called on before she did. The smell of chalk settled in the dusty old halls of McCoy Elementary. The steam heaters hissed and fogged up the tall windows. Whenever Paige thought of school, she saw chalk, milk through a straw, and water from a drinking fountain. Paige also learned that if she was working in a group, and came up with an idea or knew the answer first, Mrs. Ward, the white kindergarten teacher, would give the credit to a little white boy named Bobby.

One day, when Paige had suffered enough sabotage from this thief of her ideas, she caught him in the coat room and socked him in the nose. When Bobby's nose began to bleed, Paige gave him one of her mittens to wipe away the crimson blood. Somehow, his blood and tears got mingled on her tongue, as she spit on her other mitten, in an attempt to clean the child up.

"What's going on?" Paige heard Mrs. Ward say from behind Bobby's head. The little coat room only had one exit, and Paige would have to bulldoze around Mrs. Ward's plump girth to get out of it.

"She did it," Bobby said, pointing to Paige.

Before Paige could sputter out a lie, she was half-dragged, half-marched to the front of the room. With the whole class looking on, Mrs. Ward turned her upside down and paddled away. All Paige could see spinning in her head was blood, tears, and Bobby's snot.

Paige never remembered how she got home. All she knew was the blinding sting and blazing humiliation burning in her heart.

"Mama! Mama!" Paige couldn't wait to get to the sanctuary of home. Once in the citadel of Jewel's arms, Paige demanded that Jewel go stand up to the Goliath of her five-year-old world — the latest bully in her life.

"What's the matter, Baby?"

"Mama, go beat the teacher up. She hit me. I'm never going back to school, again."

"I can't hit the teacher, Baby. What did you do?"

Page could not explain all of her frustration at being snubbed or overlooked. She did not know how to form the words yet to explain how she had left a world where everyone called her "Baby" to infiltrate a hostile world. All of her teachers were white. It seemed that the world apart from 539 Cottrow was peopled by gargoyles, who treated the little white girls, with straight hair like dogs, with reverence. Paige knew that she had the same hands, feet, and eyes she'd always had, but she sensed that the world saw something beyond her that was wrong.

Since Paige had no words for the bruises on her spirit or the blood seeping out of the castle of her self-love as the holes in her defenses were so battered, she spent the afternoon crying.

But somehow, Paige could not seem to learn the lessons of the white world that easily. She had always seen a story-book picture portrayed on television, yet she knew it didn't reflect anything she saw in the environment around her, but the problem came when she had to interact with this foreign world. It was like getting jumbled up in jimsonweeds.

Shortly after that incident, Paige came home from school crying again. Only this time, it was because of her brothers, Danny and Joey.

Until Paige started school, she had not really known the difference in texture in black hair and white hair. From watching Shirley Temple tap dance away with Bill "Bojangles" Robinson, she only knew that Shirley's hair looked different than the plaits she and her friends wore.

When she first touched the little white girls' hair in her class, she realized that this hair was different. Sort of like the fur on the honey-colored cocker spaniel they had named Blondie. Not "good" or "bad," but different.

Later, observing the nods of approval and smiles of encouragement that Miss Ward and the other children gave to these little white girls, Paige realized that the world put a value on this hair.

Since she still had the vestiges of babyhood, love, and acceptance warming the penumbra of her edges, she intuitively understood that her hair was beautiful, also. Paige decided to take her hair down and let it flow loose and long. Paige didn't care if unbraided, her hair was only about two inches long. The sides stayed so stubby her friends called her "Naps on the Side."

But that didn't matter. Hadn't Mama said she was a little princess?

"Bald headed," Joey hissed from his fifth grade line, as his class filed through the hallway at school, passing Paige's line.

"Nappy headed," Danny teased, when he saw her from his second grade line.

Paige didn't even have to run home to tell Jewel. Danny and Joey beat her to it.

"Mama, Baby up there embarrassing me. Walking

around school with her little short hair standing all over her head."

"Yeah," Joey added, "Mama, she looked like Buck Wheat."

Buck Wheat was the little colored boy with the braids sticking up all over his head featured every Saturday on the television show, "The Little Rascals."

For Jewel, both of her girls' heads of hair were a source of frustration. With the boys, all she had to do was keep their hair cut short and brushed. With the girls, she had to struggle to try to catch up their hair in a braid. For one thing, no one had hardly ever taken any time with her hair when she was a child, so until she was able to press her hair and braid it herself, her hair had never been nicely cared-for as a little girl.

Because her girls cried so whenever she pressed their hair, she would only warm comb the top half and leave the back of their hair in its natural state. Generally, the hair of both Paige's and Midge's girlfriends looked as shiny as patent leather shoes after their mothers washed and straightened it. However, Jewel's girls' hair always had the dull sheen of a Senegalese jungle.

When Jewel saw how heartbroken Paige was over what her brothers had said, she told her, "Don't worry. You're Mama's little blue-eyed princess. Your hair is long to me. You look like Shirley Temple to me."

As mischievous as the wind itself, Paige climbed trees, ran like a boy, and stayed in trouble at school. But what amazed Jewel most was how quickly the child picked up words and loved to read and be read to from picture books. Jewel, for the first time in fifteen years, had a five year old without a baby or two underneath and underfoot. She would always read to the older children from the Bible, and occasionally take them to the library, but she'd never had the time to just read to any of the other children, one-on-one, by themselves.

Perhaps because of this, one day Jewel took Paige by the hand and caught the street car to the library in the white area of Delray. This became the start of their special time alone. All Paige could think of was how Mama had the softest hands in the world, as she held her hand while they climbed aboard the trolley. On the way home, waiting to catch the street car, Mama talked about her dreams to Paige.

"I want you to have a coming-out party when you become a young lady, Baby."

"What's that, Mama?"

"Something real nice. I saw it in a magazine."

"I want you to take music lessons, too. Maybe we'll start you on piano."

"I don't want to play no piano."

"Well, you hear those albums I play. That's classical music. That's what I want you to like."

Paige didn't reply. She thought of how her mother liked to listen to Tchaikovsky and Mozart on their stereo.

She just wished her mother was like everybody else's mother in the neighborhood. Why did her mother have to act so different?

When Paige turned eight, she began to round up a group of friends and the little band of children would venture on foot into the white neighborhood to visit the library. One afternoon, Paige, Smokey, their other girl friend, Lee Esther, and Fat Charles, Lee Esther's younger brother, had walked to the library. It was a blustery November day where the wind had wrapped itself around the earth like a spinning top. The wind swept the sky clean of clouds. It was so windy that while the children checked out their books, the bay windows of the library rattled. The wind roared, wailed, and moaned, reminding Paige of the story of "The Three Billy Goats Gruff."

Fat Charles began to cry. "I want to go home to my mama. I'm scared."

"See, that's why I didn't want to bring you with me in the first place," his sister, Lee Esther, fussed. "Always whining. And look at you. Done messed in your pants again. I'ma tell Mama. She done told you about dookeying on your stanking self."

Paige was so absorbed in the first book she had ever found in the entire library about a little colored girl like herself, that she did not take time to look up. In fact, she was so excited that she had read the entire book before she went to the white lady at the checkout counter.

"Do not bring this book back all torn up like the last time you checked out a book," Miss Anderson, the white librarian, warned Lee Esther.

"My little brother did it," Lee Esther said, pointing to Fat Charles, who was beginning to reek more and more of feces.

Paige wished she had gone to the library by herself.

"Dang, y'all ready to go all ready?"

"My Mama gon' whip me if I get home and the street lights are on," Smokey whined. "Hurry up, Paige. You always take too long when we come to the library."

By the time they left the library, it was closing time. Outside, the sun had disappeared, and the evening looked as if golden dust had been sprinkled on the earth.

"Let's run home," Paige said.

"It's all your fault," Lee Esther grumbled. "Now my Mama gonna whip me, too."

"Yeah," Smokey enjoined, "everytime Paige gets her nose in some stupid book, she can't put it down."

"Aw, just tell your mother it was story telling time at the library."

Paige didn't understand why everybody else's mother was so mean. Now, sometimes, she was glad her mother was different. For one, Mama didn't whip her as much as the other mothers whipped her friends. And another thing she liked was how Mama always made sure Paige had plenty of ice cream money, too. Then, Paige, in elaborate ceremonies of childish one-up-manship, would lick her ice cream cone in front of Lee Esther and Smokey.

One time Smokey had gotten so mad while Paige circled the ice cream in her face, chanting, "Your eyes may shine, your teeth may gritter, but none of this ice cream, you're gonna gitter," that Smokey gulped the entire head off the ice cream cone, leaving only an empty shell.

Paige was so shocked that it took her a minute to digest what had happened. That was the day Paige learned something new about Smokey. And that was the fact that Smokey could outrun her.

Screaming and crying, "I'ma get you, Smokey!" Paige

chased her friend in hot pursuit of her ice cream. Not only did Smokey outrun Paige, she was able to jump her grandmother's fence, with the scoop of ice cream lodged in her mouth like a sink stopper, the entire time.

Later that evening, Paige knocked on Miss Lenore's door.

"What is it, Baby?"

"Miss Lenore," Paige began. She was so choked up, she could hardly continue, as she fought the screen of tears flooding her eyeballs. "Smokey ate my ice cream."

Miss Lenore's face looked strange to Paige. "Okay, I'll tell Emma Jean about that."

From that day forward, Paige never flaunted her ice cream cone in front of Smokey or Lee Esther. If she bought anything when they were around, she bought penny candy so that she could split it with them.

But she noticed how whenever Lee Esther or Smokey got a nickel or a dime, they would sneak and buy an ice cream cone, so she could only get a lick.

Most of the times, though, when Lee Esther or Smokey got their nickels, they had to share their candy or ice cream with their little sisters or brothers.

Oooh! What a bother! Thank goodness she was the baby of the family! Nobody begging all the time, "Gimme sommmme."

Or, even worse, "I'ma tell Mama." The word "tell" would be dragged out like the Tarzan yell.

Paige was so busy ruminating over all the good things about being the baby of the family that she didn't notice when a large brown and black German Shepherd came racing up to the group of children. The children were taking the shortcut across the high school yard. Before they could run, the dog started jumping all over Fat Charles.

When Fat Charles began to run in a circle, the dog, close on his heels, chased him in a merry-go-round circle of motion. Looking on, Paige laughed. It looked as if the dog was playing with Fat Charles.

It was only when they heard Fat Charles' cries of pain, that the three girls began to call for help.

"Help! Help!"

But the dog would not stop attacking Fat Charles. It seemed as though the smell of human waste on Fat Charles held the same magnetic power for the dog as a bottle of Thunderbird held for Hambone, the neighborhood wino.

Finally, a white man, apparently the owner, showed up on the school ground and called the dog.

"Come here, Bobo," he said, and the dog obediently followed his owner.

It was only after the dog retreated that the children noticed that Fat Charles' pants were torn in shreds from the seat bottom to the full length of the pants' legs. Although he was not bleeding profusely, specks of blood dotted his pants. The dog had bitten Fat Charles over twenty-five times.

"Run! Go get my Mama!" Lee Esther cried out to Smokey and Paige.

The two girls ran until they made it back to the black area of Delray. When they made it to Lee Esther's house, they found her mother, Ida Belle, washing clothes in the basement. Her face was drenched in sweat. She had a look on her face that said, "If one more thing happens today —"

Yet when the girls cried out their story as to what had happened to her obese child, Ida Belle's face remained as calm as an unrippled lake.

"Where is he?" was all she asked.

"He's up on Southwest High School's playground."

The Ebony Tree

With no further questions, Ida Bell jumped into her black Cadillac and put her foot to the gas pedal.

Jewel began to do day work when Midge was twelve and Paige was five. By the time Paige was nine, Jewel had found a better job working at a Jewish Convalescent Home for the Aged on the west side of Detroit.

Gradually, even more of Jewel's house work shifted to Midge's shoulders. But by this time, Jewel was making plans to get her children out of Delray.

Meanwhile, Midge became more of a tyrant. Sixteen-year-old female caliph, she issued orders between clenched teeth. Each weekend when she deep-cleaned their bedroom, Paige was banished from the room until bed time. There was a meanness in Midge which Paige found absent in Jewel. Sometimes, because Jewel was so lenient with her, Paige obeyed and minded Midge better — as if she was the mother.

Because Paige was such an inveterate tattletale, she was the catalyst to many whippings for her older sister and brothers. Likewise, Paige was also the recipient of many fist fights with her older brothers and sister — all of which she came out the loser, but all of which only served to make her tougher.

One sweltering, pregnant-lady's nightmare day in August, when Jewel was at work, caterpillars, looking like squashed egg yolks on the sidewalk, beckoned Paige to come out to play.

Grasshoppers screamed, "It's summer. Let's play." Blue jays chased each other. But it was wash day, and Paige had to help Midge wash the family laundry. The clothes were always washed in the humid, hot dungeon of the basement. The cement blocks on the basement walls were as clammy with moisture and steam as a fecund bowl of soup on a wintry day.

Paige knew the feeling a prisoner must have. She almost felt like digging under ground and burrowing to the sapling green day outside.

Typical of a Detroit summer day, it was so muggy that rivers of sweat dripped down Midge's face. Paige sized up her sister. Four beads of sweat on her upper lip meant that Midge was not quite as evil as she usually was. She decided to test the waters.

"Midge, can I go over to Smokey's and play?" she ventured.

"We ain't through yet. Who do you think is going to hang up all these clothes?"

"Midge, you know Mama said I'm too little to be hangin' up clothes on the line. I'm only supposed to help you wring them out."

While Midge fed the clothes through the wringer washer, into the bluing water standing in the first of the two steel tubs sitting by the washer, Paige perfunctorily pulled the white sheet through the wringer.

"Well, I started hanging up clothes at nine. It's about time you start helping around here more. You see all this work Mama got to do with all these trifling niggers around here. Hmpph. You just as pure D trifling as they are. Always laying around reading or writing some stupid stories. All of you're just pathetic. You especially, Paige. You're just the epitome of triflingness."

Midge liked to try out big words to feel mature. She was sixteen, but she considered herself grown. Underneath she envied how Paige could get absorbed in a book or write stories. Even though she was graduating a year early and was going to be class valedictorian, Midge never liked to read like Paige did.

She didn't see what Paige saw in reading. She was more practical minded. Besides, look how lazy that Paige was. Now that Danny had a paper route, Paige washed most of the dishes. That girl left more grease and food on the dishes than she left swirling around in the dish water. And another thing. She couldn't stand rooming with that pig. Paige's side of the room looked a mess. Well, today, Midge was going to break up all of this laziness.

As Midge's tirade rained on her head, Paige didn't say anything. Her mind was churning with ways to figure out how to get outside.

Finally, when the clothes were all washed up, and Paige had half-heartedly helped Midge hang them up, Paige had an idea.

"Can I go sit in the mulberry tree, Midge?"

Paige knew Midge would not object to her simply going in the back yard.

Languidly sitting in the bough of the mulberry tree, shaded by the canopy of leaves, Paige snapped off a branch and pretended to smoke a cigarette while she thought about her next move. Ordinarily, the mulberry tree was where she liked to go and read or day dream. She liked to pretend the bough was her tree house. Because she had climbed up the trunk of the tree so much, it was beginning to lose its bark and looked like the worn-out knees in a pair of corduroy pants.

Paige studied a fat yellow caterpillar with a black stripe through it. The caterpillar chewed through a leaf, making a hole in it. She gazed at an army of ants as they built a house at the base of the tree. Now even ants had sense, she decided. She had seen them build bridges over water puddles. She had watched them carry pieces of bread meant for the birds to their camps. Wasn't she smarter than an ant?

Paige climbed out of the tree and went and sat in front of the screen door on the back porch. Midge had just started cooking dinner in the kitchen, which had a direct view to the front and back doors. Paige sighed loudly. Next, she hung her head on her neck, looking like a sick, melancholic dog. It worked.

"Get out of here," Midge's voice said from behind her, above her head. Paige never looked back she was running so fast. She just wanted to be sure Midge did not change her mind. Paige didn't know that what had moved Midge to pity was the memory of how Midge had felt when she was little. She never forgot the yearning she'd had to go outside to play, but she had always been tied down with a little brother or sister. Midge could never remember being free to be a child. She didn't want Paige to suffer the same fate, even though she felt Paige was a little too wild.

The first thing Paige did was round up Smokey and Lee Esther. Smokey's mother, Miss Lenore, used to live across the street from Paige's family, but they had moved into a two-bedroom apartment with their five children. Since both of her friends now lived across the hall from each other in the apartment building at the corner of Cottrow and South Bend, the two girls' mothers had become good friends. Sometimes, Paige wished her mother had friends in the neighborhood — people whom Jewel could holler at, "Aw Ida Belle, I got it!" like the time when Miss Lenore first learned how to do the new dance craze, "The Twist." But Jewel never danced. She never laughed. She always looked serious.

When the girls hung on the street pole — their usual

meeting place—they were at a loss for what to do. The day was frocked in the green and gold of high summer, yet a certain ennui had overcome them. Idleness and boredom gave birth to a desire to experience high adventure.

"Y'all seen Scratchy lately?" Paige asked.

"Yeah," Smokey said. "There he go up in the window."

Smokey took that moment to hurl a threat up toward the opened window on the second floor of the apartment building.

"I'ma beat your butt, Scratchy, when you come outside."

Scratchy had moved into the apartment building one month earlier. Because he cried and cowered in fear when he was picked on, each day someone picked a fight and beat him up. It was as though everyone had found someone who could make even the weakest coward feel powerful. Scratchy brought the beast out in all the children.

"Scratchy, I heard you was talking about my Mama," Lee Esther, hands forming a horn, yodeled up at the boy. Feeling safe in the confines of his home, and knowing his sister, Judy, had recently beaten up a gang of girls for picking on him, Scratchy stuck out his tongue.

"Scratchy, I'm a beat your butt so bad you're gonna look like a bowl of potato salad," Paige catcalled.

After a while, the three girls tired of sticking their fingers up in bad-word signs at Scratchy.

Whaticka dodicka yaldicka wantidka todidka dodicka?" Smokey asked in their secret language version of Pig Latin.

"Let's don't talk Pig Talk, today." Paige vetoed this idea.

"Why don't you write some stories for us to act out?" Lee Esther suggested.

Lee Esther scratched a circle in the dirt with her worn-out tennis shoe.

"Naw, let's go to the playground and play horse shoes or root the peg," Smokey said, since she liked going to the playground.

"Root the peg" involved flipping an ice pick into the soft dirt from the head, from the shoulders, from the elbow, and finally at waist height. Each time the pick landed and pierced the sandy loam, the player got another turn.

"Naw, we did that yesterday," Paige said, as an idea germinated in her head.

She had just finished reading *Tom Sawyer* and she liked all the adventures he and *Huck Finn* had.

"Why don't we go swipe some of Ol' Man Turner's grapes?"

"Remember when Lenny Boo-Boo's mother hit us in the head with the broom for stealing her grapes," Smokey recalled.

Just the memory had the girls rolling with glassy-eyed laughter, clasping arms, and leaning on each other.

"Yeah," Paige remembered. "She had the nerve to come telling my big sister on me. Followed me home with the broom still in her hand."

Paige put her hands on her slim hips and rolled her eyes as she often saw Midge do when she felt something was "pathetic."

Paige didn't bother to tell her friends how, although Midge had not told Jewel what had happened, she had whipped her with a belt.

Lee Esther and Smokey, trusting Paige's vivid imagination to provide them with adventure, agreed to go ransack the Turner grapevine.

An hour later, when they were chased out of the Turner grape arbor, laughing and racing the wind, they became bored again. The sun splotched their arms and legs with laces of tree leaves.

Sauntering out of the alley, "dip walking" as they called their special stride, their shadows mimicked young trees, bending and swaying in the wind.

For a while, the girls entertained themselves with grape peel fights. Just about the time that activity was winding down, they saw a horse-drawn milk carriage. It was The Milk Man.

"Hey, let's go get some ice off the truck," Paige yelled.

"Yeah."

"Give us some ice, Mr. Milkman," they all begged at once, running along the side of the truck.

"Get away from this truck, you little niggers!"

The truck driver generally gave them a chip of ice on a scorching day like this, but today he was too hot and bothered himself.

"Aw, shut up," Paige retorted, starting an undertow of defiance.

"Go to hell," Smokey joined in on the wave of belligerence.

"Kiss my ass," Lee Esther crested the wave.

"Forget him. Later for that ice."

Paige, crashing onto the shores of acceptance, decided to leave the matter alone. She had another prank up her sleeve. She pulled out a cigarette and a book of matches she'd filched out of her mother's purse that morning. Walking away from the truck, she lit it and took a puff.

Blowing a smoke ring, Paige handed the cigarette over to Lee Esther.

Neither Paige nor Lee Esther heard Smokey when she whispered, "Let's get a ride on the back of the truck."

By the time Paige turned around, the first thing she noticed was how the sun glinted on Smokey's vaselined, dusky skin. Everything seemed to happen in slow motion after that. Time became a syrupy stream of molasses, dripping from a narrow spigot. Nothing could make time budge its crippled toes.

Looking on, as if in a trance, Lee Esther and Paige watched Smokey swing off the same hook that the milkman swung his lithe body from each morning, day after day, as he delivered everyone their milk. Only, somehow, Smokey didn't land deftly onto the pavement with both feet as the milkman did. Instead Smokey's right foot slipped off the side board, causing her to trip to the newly-asphalted street. The back right wheel caught the big toe of her tennis shoe first, then her entire foot.

Thus pinned in, Smokey could not get loose. Just like Tar Baby, she was trapped, and the more she tried to get free, the more entangled she became. Before anyone could tell the driver to stop—before it actually registered to any of the three girls what was taking place—the back right wheel began to run over the backside of Smokey's right toe, ankle, then her heel. Slowly, the wheel traveled up the back of her lower leg, across the back of her thigh, and over her entire eight-year-old torso. Finally, with the slow dullness of a baby's head crowning from the birth canal, the full weight of the truck heaved, hesitated as though stuck, then mercilessly crunched over Smokey's small skull. It sounded just like when Paige's older brother, Judge, cracked his knuckles. Crunch. Crunch. Crunch.

Smokey never cried out. Her mouth opened in a big "O," as if she were simply observing an ant carrying a piece of bread to its hole.

Time stopped. Earth, trees, and manholes spun around and around for what seemed like a bottomless whirlpool of minutes. Paige tried to cry out, but she only heard her voice shout inside her head.

Time held at abeyance, she stood, gaping, for what seemed like hours. Finally, she found her voice.

"Lee Esther! Run and get help!"

Lee Esther, whose legs were as thin as celery stalks, ran like a narrow locomotive train, screaming, "Mama! Help! Smokey been runned over by a milk truck! Miss Lenore! Come quick! Smokey hurt!"

Finally, Paige managed to unglue herself from the hot pavement. She ran over and helped Smokey off the ground.

"I can't walk!" Smokey garbled. Her speech sounded like a slip of a needle on a .78 record when Paige would slow the speed down.

"Put your arm around my shoulder," Paige told her. "Lean on me."

The truck finally came to a halt, and out jumped the young white driver.

"What the hell!" was all he could say. A woman named Miss Garnet came running out with a white towel to put around Smokey's neck. "I seen everything, Mister. Why didn't you stop? You knew you were running over this child."

"Miss, I had no way of knowing. One minute she was asking me for ice, and the next thing I knew, I heard a thump."

A yellow pus, streaked with slimy strings of blood, dribbled out of Smokey's mouth. "My Mama gon' whip me," she mumbled over and over. Her words came out as if she had rocks in her mouth.

What followed seemed to happen like a slow ballet under water. Frozen to the spot where she stood, Paige slapped at a mosquito on her lower leg. Her socks had crawled down inside her tennis shoes. She didn't bother to stoop and pull up her socks.

Paige could only look on in a daze as Lee Esther and Miss Lenore, Smokey's mother, ran to the scene of the accident. Miss Ida Belle, Lee Esther's mother, was close on their heels. Paige was equally amazed at how neither woman seemed to panic. Their bronzed faces were immobile, stoic. As if they could and would accept whatever fate dealt out. Miss Ida Bell had already buried a nineteen-year-old son last year. Hurled over nineteen feet into the air, Joe had been struck and killed by an automobile. Miss Lenore's stepmother, Millie, had been knifed to death by her boyfriend six years earlier in a horrendous crime of passion. Neither woman was a stranger to death or its companion, loss. Through living, they had learned to accept pain and suffering as a part of this earthly sojourn. They both wore the robes of endurance as majestically as mink wraps.

In the distance, Paige heard the approaching sirens of an ambulance. People began to flood into the street. They spilled out of houses in droves and swarms. Nothing ever happened in Delray that did not draw out a crowd and warrant gossip. A magnet in and of itself, bad news drew people like spoiled meat attracted flies. And people feasted on tragedy.

Grown people had no place to go, no money to spend, and nothing to do. It was just as easy to become involved in children's affairs, as well as it was to get in grown folk's business. People loved to sit and gossip on their porches. The somnolent day had been pierced by this event. Now people had found something to suckle their teeth on. The story grew with the telling of it, as word-of-mouth news traveled at the speed of a thunderbolt. Better still, it was fresh off the press from the grapevine of small talk, so no one had to get warmed-over news.

"Miss Lenore and Lionel's gal been hit by a milk truck."

"Mmmm-mmh. I seen the whole thing."

"Hear tell that kid of Jewel's pushed her off the truck."

Because no one was close to Jewel, no one understood her. Because they didn't understand her, they disliked her. Like most people, they hated what they could not understand. Because everyone accepted Miss Lenore as one of them, their sympathy rose for her poor little dark daughter.

"You know the dark child."

"Yeah, the pretty jet black one?"

After the ambulance whisked Smokey off to Children's Hospital, which the milk company would later pay for, along with the hospital bill, Paige moped around the rest of the day. When she stumbled home, still in shock, she didn't tell anyone what had happened. Jewel was at work at her new job at the Jewish Home for the Aged. Since she took two buses home, she usually didn't get home from work until about ten o' clock at night.

Around eight o' clock that evening, when the sun was just beginning to bow its flaming, pomegranate head, a knock came at the front door. It was the storekeeper, Miss Coretta.

"Is your mother home?" she asked Midge.

Midge hesitated. She was used to lying to the Insurance Man, the Watkins man, and the Milk Man. She had learned never to volunteer any information to adults.

"Why? Is something the matter?"

Midge knew her mother didn't like Miss Coretta, but she did not know why.

"Well, I just came to tell her what I saw from my store window. Did you know Miss Lenore's daughter, Emma

Jean, was hit by a milk truck today? Mmmmh. And I saw the whole thing from my store. That little sister of yours pushed her off the milk truck and caused her to get ran over, too."

Paige was standing by the kitchen door listening.

"Paige, come here." Midge had a flat expression on her face, so Paige couldn't tell if she was mad or not.

She sure hoped she didn't try to whip her like the time when Lenny Boo Boo's mother had followed her home with the broom. Paige went sheepishly into the living room.

"Did you do that Paige?"

"No, I didn't." Paige couldn't believe grown-ups could fib so. "I helped Smokey over to the sidewalk."

"Are you calling me a liar, young lady?"

Paige stared back at Miss Coretta with brazen brown eyes, but did not answer. Miss Coretta was known for cheating everyone who came into her Mom and Pop store. She set the meat scales higher than any of the other neighborhood grocery store owners. With a child's unerring instinct, Paige knew that Miss Coretta was poison ivy. She infected everything and everyone she touched.

"Well, I just thought you needed to know and tell your mother."

Miss Coretta turned on her heels and left in a huff.

Even after Smokey recovered and was released from the hospital, Midge never whipped Paige. And if she ever told Jewel what had happened, Jewel never mentioned it to Paige.

There were so many words locked inside of Jewel's head, it scared her sometimes. What she'd discovered from early life was that words were accouterments which just tripped life's feet. People said they loved you and hurt you. People said they were coming back to get you and didn't show up for thirteen years.

She'd seen the verb "love" become as mangled as the shackles her ancestors had worn. Love had found its home in a wine bottle. Love in the juke joints. So words just became contraband in her vocabulary. They were the Bermuda Triangle of her personality she didn't tread into lightly. When Jewel spoke, she measured her words.

Mostly, she sang snatches of a tuneless melody — she never quite finished because she didn't remember all the words — while she went about her work.

> *Nobody knows the trouble I've seen,*
> *Nobody knows but Jesus. . .dall-dall*
> *Trouble of the world. . .*

Besides, what was there to say? Did old Father Sun talk his business while he went about warming the universe? She only wished her kids didn't ask so many questions.

"Mama, when we gon' move from Delray?"

"Mama, what's wrong with you? Why you always fussing at Daddy? He didn't do nothing. He be mindin' his own business."

Even when Solly cooked and had her dinner on the table, she was seared by anger.

"Look, Daddy just be roasting peanuts. I'm tired of you fussing at my Daddy."

Jewel was nearly floored the day she heard Paige say this. When Paige started crying, she was befuddled. She'd never felt that Paige was as close to Solly as Midge was, so from then on, she tried not to argue as much in front of the children.

If only the children knew of the well of frustration she felt. She hated working outside of the home. Hated the long hours of being away from her children. Just to come home and look at Solly idling away when he was laid-off was enough to send her into paroxysms of anger. . . .But she would do whatever it took to keep her kids from growing up on welfare as a way of life. The last time Jewel stood in line for four hours at the public assistance office, she said to herself, no more. She told herself, "Jewel, see if you can get yourself some days' work."

At first Jewel had found several days of "day work" cleaning for a white family named Stole. The family had a little boy named Robby, and they had given Paige his boy bike. With Paige being such a tomboy, she didn't seem to mind riding a boy's bike. Often when Jewel would get off the bus, she would see Paige riding Robby's old bike, along with two of her friends — one on the handlebars and one on the bar across the center — wobbling dangerously from side to side. The Stole family also gave her plenty of clothes for herself and her children.

About four years later, Jewel left Mrs. Stole's house for the convalescent home. Although the Stoles had grown crazy about Jewel — how quiet and clean she was — they wished her well when she decided to leave.

Jewel had looked in the newspaper and found the convalescent home job. It was located on the west side of town. The only thing she hated was she had to work on Jewish Holidays, as well as Easter Sundays. That was the first Easter she was not at home to see a bonneted and gloved Paige off to Sunday School. Despite the fact it took two hours each way on the bus, she made forty dollars every two weeks and that was the most money she'd ever made. Within six months, Jewel had been able to wallpaper her living room and reupholster her sectional sofa set. She'd bought Danny a brand new racer bike, and Paige a violin. The violin was brand new and had cost Jewel one hundred dollars. But Paige would be able to take free lessons at school. Jewel was determined that at least one of her six children was going to take music lessons.

Once, two years earlier, she'd sent Midge and Paige to one piano lesson, but found that she couldn't afford the second one, so they had stopped going to music lessons. It never occurred to Jewel that she couldn't afford a piano. She just figured a way would be made out of no way, as it usually was. Well, the school gave these violin lessons free, so Jewel wouldn't have to worry about paying for them. Whenever she looked at the violin, Jewel's face beamed with pride. Just its burnt sienna body, curved like a miniature voluptuous woman, gave visions of future ecstasy. And once Paige began to play its reedlike, whiny notes with different orchestras from various high schools, no matter if she had to work, Jewel made sure she was present in the audience. Not only did she have dreams of Paige being a child prodigy, she liked to be present to get glimpses into the eternity that symphony music provided for her. Within her first year of working at the convalescent home, she'd been able to pinch away a little

149

money in order to get her children out of Delray. Already, Cake Sandwich and Judge had graduated from high school and gone into the service, yet she was still living in Delray. She was determined that she was not going to see anymore of her children raised up in Delray.

That was what she was thinking that particular night when November's windy beak snatched at her thin coat tail, whipped up her dress hem, and exposed her knotted stockings above her knobby knees. Assaulted by the night winds, huddled turtle-like, Jewel rubbed her hands together. She had not worn any gloves, and her hands felt like bricks.

Ordinarily, Jewel and sixteen-year-old Midge took turns wearing the same black wool coat. Tonight it was her turn to wear it. Since Midge didn't have to go to school, Jewel wore the coat when she was working on the weekends. Her feet were so cold, that Jewel regretted she hadn't worn her boots, even if they did leak. Jewel was running behind schedule.

Earlier that night, she'd had a difficult time with an elderly, shriveled man named Percy Weinstein. After changing his diaper, and getting his withered little body strapped into bed, Jewel was tired. Lord, Jewel hoped she never had to be old and burdensome like Percy. She always felt sorry for this old man in particular, because no one ever came to see him.

"I like you coloreds," he told Jewel on one of his more lucid days. "When I was a little boy, we had a maid named Mable. Best maid we ever had. Clean. Honest, too. She was so nice to me, I wished she could have stayed with us all the time. Then, her mother went blind, and she said she had to quit. Said she had to be with her mother. Not like my people. Not like my people...." Percy's voice drifted off.

Jewel felt so sorry for Percy. No one ever came to visit him. She wondered when she got old, if her children would put her in an old folks home. She shivered. It was just too dismal to think about.

That particular night, Percy had been especially cantankerous.

"Call my son," he had said over and over.

"Okay," Jewel said. "But not until you take your medicine."

"Tell my son, I want him to bring me some Kosher food. He knows I'm not supposed to eat Gentile foods."

Jewel finally got him to take his medicine, and Percy was able to fall off to sleep. Jewel waited until he was snoring, before she left the room. After she left the convalescent home, Jewel felt a heaviness around her heart.

Percy reminded her of Mama Lovey and how she'd died. Nonetheless, Mama Lovey's death had been different.

For one, Mama Lovey had died in the same bed in which she'd given birth to her eighteen children. She'd kept the same dresser bureau, the same mirror, and the same slop jar in her room all of her married life. These familiar fixtures were the last earthly sights she'd set her eyes on. Most of all, Mama Lovey hadn't died alone. Like Percy would. Still, Jewel wondered had Mama Lovey ever gotten what she'd wanted out of life? Had she died angry when she took her last breath?

Engrossed so deep in thought, Jewel didn't make it to her bus stop at her usual time. Just as she turned the corner, she saw her regular bus retreating. She let out a sigh of disgust. It was already dark. The streets were empty, save for the dead leaves which swirled and scurried around her feet. The full moon painted a leery eye in the heavens, making Jewel's flesh prickle. Although the streets were bathed in moon light, they were empty.

Jewel instinctively held her purse close to her bosom. She'd just gotten paid and usually pinned her money inside of her brassiere. She was so perturbed over Percy that she'd absently placed the money in her purse that night. She knew it would be another hour before the last bus of the night ran up Livernois Street. She was tired. How would she make it another three hours?

To pass time, Jewel began to mentally add up all the things she had to do with her pay. Jewel needed boots herself, but so did Paige. Danny was growing like a weed and needed new pants. She couldn't remember when she'd last had a new dress. She tried to keep the one house dress she wore around the house clean. Thank God, she wore a uniform to work with her white crepe-soled shoes. She washed it out every other night. Often, Jewel didn't wear panties because she had none. She remembered that her washing machine was broken again, and she was going to have to wash in the tub for the six of them still at home.

When something began to tug at her lower arm, Jewel's first instinct was to bend her elbow and pull her arms up to the shoulder straps of her purse.

"What's going on?" She hadn't the slightest idea for at least several seconds that the young man, no more than nineteen — Cake Sandwich's age — was trying to snatch her purse. She was being attacked!

The young man was dressed in a dark lumber jacket. He wore a wool knitted cap pulled down over his forehead. His eyes and mouth were barely visible. Because of his closeness, Jewel could smell his breath. It reeked of alcohol.

Once the fact registered in her brain, Jewel got angry. "Hey, let go of my purse!"

"Give me that purse!" The young attacker must have felt that if he growled, she would easily release the purse and its contents to him. He had also expected that Jewel, alone on a street at night like this, would be easy prey.

A month earlier, a nurse, working the graveyard shift, had been knifed to death. It was an incident which started a tidal wave of hysteria among women all over the city. Although he wasn't the murderer, the crime had worked to this petty thief's advantage. In the past week alone, he'd been able to snatch six purses without a fight, because his victims had been so afraid for their lives.

But this woman was different. This woman, who had seemed so distracted and tired, all of a sudden seemed to have developed the strength of two men. All Jewel could think of was how hard-earned her pay was. All the diapers she had changed for the past two weeks. How this little thug hadn't lifted a finger to earn it. How she had four kids still at home counting on her to help feed them.

"Oh, no you don't, nigger!" The adrenaline made her blood pump through her veins like a gushing fire hydrant.

The young man was still holding on to her purse, but Jewel used her free right hand to sock and pinch him. They struggled over the sidewalk to a patch of grass. The young man lost his balance and tripped backwards over a stone in the grass. Once he fell, Jewel kicked and kicked at him as he covered his head. She didn't know where the strength came from, but she felt a sense of satisfaction as she lashed out. No longer would the world kick her about.

No, you take this, World. Yeah, Life. You've kicked and stomped me when I was a child, when I was down having my babies, but I'm up on my feet now. I might have been down, but I have never been all the way out.

"Please! Stop! I'll leave you alone."

Jewel still did not stop. No, Life. Do you ever stop when I say "Enough?"

No. You just keep dragging my tired time with you downstream. Well, tonight, I'm swimming back up stream, you hear, Life. It's my turn!

The young man somehow managed to stumble to his feet and scramble away. He had let go of the purse strap, long before Jewel let go of him. He was bleeding from the mouth. Looking back, when he made it safely to the corner, he half-sobbed, "Woman, you crazy!"

"Don't you ever try this on any other woman. You hear? If I even hear about it, I'll find you myself and the next time you might not be so lucky."

Jewel went into a phone booth, holding a rock, as she waited for her bus. She was too riled up over the nerve of that young punk thinking he was going to take her little money and walk away to tell about it. Before Jewel knew it, the bus had arrived.

Aunt Sunday wasn't a mean person by nature. But after twenty-five years of marriage to Uncle Jake, she'd grown as small-spirited as a caged canary. Years of never being able to please Jake, — from his fried chicken to his cherry-flavored tobacco, — had left Sunday as tightly-strung as a finely-tuned watch.

Sometimes, when Jake would get mad — she had burnt the chicken — he would kick her in the legs, then go off in a huff. Although Jake never said it, he held it against Sunday that she couldn't bear him any children.

When Jake heard that his niece, Rachel, whose husband had been in Korea for two years, had given birth to a baby by an "outside man," he had not given it a second thought. The following summer he and Sunday drove to Tulsa, Oklahoma, just as they did every summer, to visit their respective relatives. Jake liked to show off his shiny new Buick which he bought every year, so that his people could see how rich and prosperous he was.

While visiting his family, Uncle Jake heard that Rachel's husband, Linnard, was home from Korea. The couple had all ready had three children before Linnard even went into the service.

When the cuckolded husband came home from war, the "outside" baby, Claudette, was almost a year old. It was 1953. Because Linnard was mistreating Claudette so much, Rachel asked Jake if he and Sunday could take the baby for a while.

Through a tacit agreement, it was decided that Sunday and Jake would take baby Claudette back to the city and raise her until some uncertain date in the future, when the child might return to her own family. By then, Rachel, in an attempt to mend the breech with her husband, was pregnant again, with her fifth child.

Whether or not she had ever acknowledged it, Sunday had wanted a baby for years. Having had the misfortune of being born sterile, she had watched Jewel spit out baby after baby like watermelon seeds. So even though she talked about "how stupid Jewel was to keep having babies," in her heart, she envied the relative ease with which Jewel conceived and delivered her babies.

Sunday had always treated Jewel's children in a loving manner. The Shepherds had even stayed with Sunday and Jake, when Jewel first arrived in Detroit with four babies. Aunt Sunday had been especially fond of Midge. She noticed how Jewel lavished all of her attention on the boys and had tried to make up by taking Midge off Jewel's hands as much as possible. She loved how precocious Midge was.

"Aunt Sunday, I got big legs like yours," Midge chirped one day when she was three years old. But after the arrival of Claudette, why Jewel's children were the farthest things from her mind. Her days — which had formerly been arid, winding deserts — were now filled with frilly dresses to sew. Since she was fifty-one years old, she'd already gone through the change of life and having a baby was like being a young woman all over again. Jake had long since abandoned the favors of Sunday's bed in pursuit of his own separate room, so Claudette filled a long, deep need within Sunday.

The only dark spot on the advent of Claudette in Sunday's life was Paige, Jewel's youngest child. Every summer her sister, Luralee, came to Detroit from Tulsa, she had to insist on dragging that bad little devil, Paige, with her. As far as Aunt Sunday was concerned, Paige was too rough with Claudette. But Claudette, who was one year Paige's junior, seemed to dote on Paige.

The summer of sixty-one, Aunt Sunday, knowing how she harbored this secret disdain for Paige, reluctantly agreed to allow the child, along with Danny, to take a train trip to Tulsa, Oklahoma with her and Claudette. That summer Jake wasn't going, because he had to work.

The trip came about for Paige by her making Jewel feel guilty.

One day Jewel was pressing Paige's hair. For Paige, this was already a source of bimonthly torture, but she had something festering inside of her. Suddenly, the child broke into tears.

"What's the matter?" she asked.

Between sobs, Paige choked out the words, "I'm the only one who never been on a trip."

"Who said that?"

"Danny. He was teasing me. He said yall didn't take me on no trips 'cause I was left on the door step."

The truth was, the only trip Danny had gone on himself was a long car ride to Oakland, California with Solly and Uncle A.J. to help bury another brother, named Lennie, in 1957.

Although Jewel was not one for always taking to heart what her children moaned and groaned about not having, because she couldn't do any better, she always felt a little guilty about Paige.

Often, she didn't discipline the child enough, because she was proud of her spunk and spirit. Although Paige was a bit sassy, Jewel was glad she hadn't taught her to say, "M'am," which was so country to her. She had never wanted Paige to be as cowered down as she had been as a child. From the age of eight, Paige wrote stories and illustrated them herself. Paige had even taught herself to ballet from a book. And to think Jewel almost didn't have her! Not that Jewel felt guilty about that, because she had only done what she had to do.

But sometimes, it bothered Jewel that she'd missed out on the first three years of Paige's life through depression. So with Paige, Jewel tended to spoil her. Also, with her working long hours, Jewel could see what a street urchin Paige was becoming. That made her feel sorry for the child. She'd always been at home when the older children were coming up.

When Luralee asked if Danny and Paige could go to Tulsa with Aunty Sunday on the train, but spend two weeks between the different relatives' homes, Jewel had agreed. She regretted that she had never gone anywhere as a child, herself.

For two weeks, she would not have to worry about Paige roaming up and down the street. Later, when her in-laws from California showed up unexpectedly, she was really glad she'd let Paige and Danny go, so there was more room to bed her company down in. Plus, it hadn't helped matters that her washing machine was out again, so once more, Jewel was washing on a scrub board in the tub.

Jewel did not have an inkling that Aunt Sunday secretly envied her for having children. Judging from outward appearances, Sunday's life looked picture-book perfect to Jewel. Nice new furniture. A brick house. Glossy hardwood floors.

Nor did she know that Sunday envied her own sister, Jewel's mother, Luralee for her independence—her leaving her husband when she had two babies. Aunt Sunday was afraid to leave Jake and she had no babies before she started raising Claudette. But because Aunt Sunday had never worked, she was totally dependent on Jake, so she, like most human beings, preferred to stay in the known comfort of Hades, than venture to the unknown bottom of Heaven.

*   *   *   *   *

In the life of a child, a day can be as long as a year. Two weeks to Paige represented the whole summer—one of her childhood memories that would always linger like moldy dustballs in the attic of her mind.

The first incident which alerted Paige that something was wrong—or either not all the way right—was when she, Danny, and Claudette, gamboling on the lawn, chased lightning bugs. Paige had never seen fire flies or lightning bugs, and she was enthralled by the wondrous sight.

The little insects illuminated the dusk like red and orange stars. In the background, the drone of whippoorwills, mosquitoes, and flies filled the air.

"Let's get a jar and catch them," Danny said.

Aunt Sunday and Aunt Mercy D sat on white steel lawn chairs by the flower bed, where they had, changing their position with the shift of the sun, moved their chairs from the front porch.

Aunt Sunday, being the peremptory and older sister of the two, was saying, "No, you're wrong, Mercy D. Uncle Rooster bought his car in 1929."

Like a weaver threads the loom, the two women wove together a tapestry made of pieces of memories.

"I think you're wrong, Sunday. Didn't nobody have money in '29. That was during the Depression."

"Well, they say Uncle Caleb did up North, where he was passing for white. And now on the Hightower side of the family, it was Uncle Rooster, and our older brother, Cash, who had all the money. They say Cash went and bought that old Chevy with all cash money, too. No wonder they called him Cash."

"Well, Cash was the meanest of all of our brothers."

"Now—no. You would have had to have seen Uncle Rooster, our Daddy's oldest brother. Whew! That man

159

was so mean he would see us younger kids walking down the road in the rain coming from school and he'd drive right by. Remember the time Cousin Thed and us almost drowned, it was raining and flooding so, while we were walking from school. I know he seen us. Weren't nobody in that big car, but him and his wife, Maybelle."

"How about that old school house? The one they had in Ebenezer Baptist Church?"

"Girl, we used to walk five miles back and forth to school. Rain or shine. Papa always said girls didn't have to go to school as far as he was concerned, but Mama Lovey said we were going to get an education if it was the last thing she seen in this world. She said all of her older girls had gotten married with no schooling, like she did, but she wanted all the younger ones of us to get some book sense."

"Well, even though Sister only went to the eighth grade, she seems to have the most money of all of us."

Paige's ears perked up. She knew they were talking about her maternal grandmother, Luralee. She didn't know who this Mama Lovey was, though.

Sunday's voice dropped. "Well, at least you did get your diploma. Sister only went to the eighth grade. Sister ain't got all that much. She send all her money to Jewel and all them children. That Solly so sorry, it's a shame."

Sunday felt secure in the knowledge that Jake was about to retire from the Uniroyal Rubber Tire factory with thirty-five years of service. "You know, I don't mean to brag, but I got the best house up in Detroit. It's all brick. That's one thing I can say about Jake, he is hard working."

Aunt Mercy D was quiet for a while. "Claudette is getting to be a big girl. You tell her about her mother and them yet?"

"Yes, I told her. That Paige—she is so onery—last year she told Claudette that there was no Santa Claus and had my child brokenhearted. So I said to myself, if Sister came to Detroit to visit this year, she'd probably be dragging that kid with her, so I thought I better tell her first."

"What did she say?"

"Say she wants to meet them."

"You're going to take her with you over to Rachel's?"

"Yes. I don't have any choice now. I had wanted to wait before I told her. But to be on the safe side — well, one thing, if I had a kid like Paige, I don't know what I would do. I don't know how Jewel puts up with that kid. She is just so mean to Claudette."

Mercy D, changing the subject as she saw Paige lingering around, asked, "Do you remember the fair of 1910?"

Playing on the lawn, the children had filled two jars of fireflies. The beetles, they'd captured were beginning to die, so Danny ran in the house to get a nail and make holes in the top of the jar.

Seamlessly, the children's games melted into playing catch.

"Let's pretend we have a ball by putting a rock inside of our socks," Danny said.   A game of hot potato ensued. Then, a game of catch.

"I got it! I got it!" cried Claudette.

"Throw it to me!" Paige shouted, the eagerness of childish abandon written all over her face.

Next, they started playing "Monkey in the Middle." Danny was the "Monkey." He had to try and catch the ball before Claudette did. Paige tossed the sock up high in the air, trying to get it over his head. The sock catapulted almost to the lamp pole. When it came down, Claudette ran to retrieve it, but couldn't catch it.

Without warning, a voice cried out in pain. It was Aunt Sunday. "What in the name of the Fathers was that?"

161

she cried.

When Paige came forth, admitting she was the culprit, it seemed as though Aunt Sunday's pain became so severe it was too unbearable for human endurance.

"What did you have in that sock—a brick?" Aunt Sunday demanded.

"No."

"Well, I demand an apology."

Although Paige apologized, she was in a quandary as to what she had done so wrong. She wondered what was the matter. After that, she tried to stay out of Aunty Sunday's way. Still, Paige began to notice that Aunt Sunday had a habit of gossiping all the time. If Aunt Mercy D and Aunt Sunday were together, Sunday talked about Paige's grandmother, Luralee. If Sunday was over at Luralee's, she talked about Mercy D. If she went to her Uncle Bubba's house, Aunt Sunday talked about Luralee and Mercy D. It didn't take Paige long to figure out that Sunday didn't like her. Also, she figured out that Sunday was the common denominator in the cauldron of talking about people behind their back. Sunday triangulated against whoever was absent when she went to visit.

It seemed that no matter what Paige did, she could not please Aunt Sunday. One afternoon Paige stumbled upon a conversation that Aunt Sunday and Aunt Mercy were having.

"I just don't deign it to be fitten to take Paige over to the Bedfords for dinner," Aunt Sunday was saying to Aunt Mercy D and her Uncle Bubba's wife, Luberta. Paige usually stayed at Luberta's or Mercy D's house while Luralee worked the afternoon shift at Greyhound bus station. The Bedfords were Luberta's next door neighbors.

Seeing Paige, Aunt Sunday changed the subject. "Do

you remember how cousin Ivy used to teach school over at the old Baptist Church?"

"Yeah," said Aunt Mercy D. "If I got in trouble, she would send a note home to Papa or Mama, and boy, would they wear us out with those switches. I hate peach trees to this day. You ain't never been beat 'til you been beat with a peach tree switch."

"Well, once Cousin Ivy sent a note home by me, and I didn't give it to Mama. You know Cousin Ivy had the nerve to come to dinner that Sunday after church just so she could tell on me."

Their voices, joined in laughter, were barbed by bittersweet pain.

"They sure were crazy back then. Daddy whipped my butt right in front of her. Look like Cousin Ivy wasn't satisfied until she saw me get that whipping."

"Mama Lovey and Papa were something else."

"I know. I sure miss them."

"Me, too," Aunt Mercy D, the baby of the family, said, wiping a tear from the corner of her eyes.

Sunday continued. "I tried to get Papa and Mama Lovey to come stay with us, but they wouldn't. Papa always pretended that he didn't have anyone to watch his hogs and cows."

"Ain't that the truth? That old man loved his farm. But couldn't nothing take the place of that old horse, Mule."

"Remember that time Mule got sick and Papa stayed up all night for three nights 'til he got him well?"

Each woman, wandering separately down her individual golden path of memory, dropped silent.

Mercy D picked back up the shuttle of the conversation and passed it to Sunday.

"And Mule weren't worth a quarter. Wouldn't work a minute pass high noon to save his horse soul."

"I think Papa liked Mule 'cause they was so much

alike."

"Remember the time Papa wouldn't pull his horse over on River Lane Bridge for the white man?"

"Yessir. Even white folks knew that Papa was crazy. And the killing part is nobody had tried to lynch him either."

"But he was crazy about him some Sister."

"I think she was his pet," Sunday said. "That's why she could drop her two kids off on him and Mama Lovey like that. They never let the older girls bring their children back home. Hear tell Sister Illy's husband was mean as a rattlesnake. Papa only said, 'A woman's place is with her husband,' when she tried to come back home. But naw. Let Sister come running back from Louisiana with two babies, and he changed that whole story. From what I recollect, Elijiah didn't beat her. She just wanted to move to Tulsa and get work.

"He had a job. Sister should've known ain't no man gon' leave his job and come following her. No. Not no real man—Paige Caldonia—if you don't stop standing around that corner looking down my throat, you better. Lord, I don't know what I was thinking when I let Sister talk me into bringing that child with me. Now Danny, he's no problem. No trouble at all. Minds his own business. Acts like a child, and he stays in a child's place. But that Paige—she too womanish for me. She act like she been here before.

"All up in grown folks business."

That evening, when Luralee picked up Paige after her afternoon shift at the bus station had ended, she asked Paige what they had eaten for dinner at the neighbor's, the Bedfords. "I didn't go to dinner with Aunt Sunday and them," Paige said, reluctantly. She was becoming more afraid of Aunt Sunday and did not want Luralee to bring it up to her sister. When Luralee was at work, she knew Aunt Sunday would take it out on her.

"Why not?"

"She said I didn't need to go."

"Did she take Claudette?"

"Yeah." Luralee had a funny look on her face, but she didn't say anything. Paige was relieved that she didn't fuss and just thought she had a stomach ache or something.

That next week, when Aunt Mercy D, Uncle Lennie, Aunt Sunday, and Claudette were planning to go to Shreveport to look over land that Mama Lovey and Papa owned, and that was being taken back by the white Hightowers for taxes, Paige thought she heard the phone ring in her dream. Paige had dozed off at Aunt Luberta's house, waiting for Luralee to come pick her up. Like a storm rumbling in her dream, she heard angry voices rise up between Aunt Sunday and someone, but she didn't know who the other person was. A while later, Paige was awakened by the angry voice of Luralee. She had never heard her grandmother sound so furious. She was arguing with Aunt Sunday, who also happened to be spending that night at Luberta's.

"Yes, you are taking Paige with you to Shreveport. I

165

don't care what you say, Sunday. If you can take her over to see Claudette's half-brothers and sisters, you can take her to see about that land."

Although Paige only had a birdseye view into what was going on between the two sisters, she felt the tension of the situation like a needle prick. When they got ready to take off for the trip, Paige had an idea. Thinking she could ease some of the anger written all over Aunt Sunday's face— which was apparent to everyone else except Claudette— when she climbed in the car, she said placatingly, "Aunt Sunday. You can sit between Claudette and me so that we can't talk too much."

Paige might as well have handed Aunt Sunday a centipede. Aunt Sunday gave Paige a scalding look meant to capture all the virulence she felt for the child.

"Hah! What do you mean? Claudette is going to lie down in the back seat so she can stretch out and sleep. You're not getting back here with me."

Mercy D, looking ashamed of her sister's vituperative venom, but also very intimidated by her, tried to appease Paige.

"Come on up here in the front with me and Uncle Lennie, Paige." Paige was crestfallen. What did she do wrong? Paige remembered how she had felt when she'd stumped her toe, walking barefoot, when she first arrived in Tulsa. She had the same scraped, stunned feeling, only now it was in the pit of her stomach.

They had left at night, and by the time Paige woke up, the sun was peeking its white head over a mountain ridge as they descended into the flatlands of Shreveport. The plains sloped gently downward. Stretches of highway, lined by cypresses and oak trees, sliced ribbon-like through the green marsh. Behind the dark gathering of trees on either side of the highway, the marsh lurked insidiously. The bayous and the swamps blew their frightening foggy breath into the air. Weeping willows dragged their mournful, hairy limbs on the ground. By noon, the fog had lifted. From her window in the front with Aunt Mercy D and Uncle Lennie, Paige watched the countryside unfurl. Cows, horses, and goats grazed in the open meadows. Wind rippled through the silky hair of cornstalks. Periwinkle sky interlaced with saffron heads of wheat. Vestiges of a morning shower washed the world in a sea of gold.

Paige saw a bull, the first one she'd ever seen in her life. She also saw her first bathrooms marked "For White Women," "For White Men," and for "colored men." The letters in the sign for colored men were all in small letters.

"Where we supposed to go to the bathroom?" Paige asked.

"Shut up," Aunt Sunday snapped. A while later, when they pulled over to a knoll of woods, Paige got out with her great-aunts and Claudette, then, she understood. The sound of the women's streams of urine sounded like gushing fire hydrants to Paige. It reminded her of the time the hydrant burst, and she and all the neighborhood children took a shower in the geyser of water.

"I wonder what Flint is doing?" Aunt Mercy D inquired of no one in particular. She was childless, and her collie, Flint, was treated like a petulant child. "Sunday, isn't that where the old Robinson place used to be?"

"No, I think that was the old Hershel place."

"Girl, I can't remember. Everything's all grown up, now. I wonder if Papa ever registered his land with the Land Assessors?"

"Well, with him not leaving a will, it'll be hard to tell. That was some valuable land. All the white people wanted it."

167

"Sunday, could you scratch my head when we get to Wilmadine's house?"

"Whoever pays the taxes own the land down here," Sunday was saying. Wilmadine was Papa's niece. She was forty-years old, big-boned, and built like a man from working in the fields. After they left her house, she drove the family back into the woods, as Lennie didn't know the back roads.

"Wilmadine can drive like a man." Uncle Lennie spoke with admiration. That was about the only words he spoke during the entire trip. Two faded shanty houses, nestled deep in the marsh, formed part of Papa's and Mama Lovey's old home. One house had a kitchen with a woodburning stove in it. The other had two rooms used for bedrooms. The two houses, which could be described more as hovels, were connected by a galley porch. An out house sat forty feet away from the house. The family used well water. Paige hated the taste of the water. It reminded her of the time Bird Bath had peed in an RC Cola bottle and offered her a swig.

"This house reminds me of the other house Papa and them owned," Sunday remarked. The two women had grown up in rural Vernon, Oklahoma, where the family relocated before they were born.

Mercy D wondered inwardly how so many of them had grown up in such a little space. And such a raggedy shack. Cobwebs looked liked they had never been swept from the ceiling. Mmmm, mmmm, mmmmh. Her two bedroom home wasn't much, but it was neat, clean, and carpeted. She'd come a long way from this little shanty.

Roaches, gnats, and flying grasshoppers inhabited every square inch of living space. Mosquitoes drank pints of Paige's blood. Pigeons flew low. Paige heard her first owl. It was as if that back road had taken them back to the turn of the century. The only modern convenience this house knew was a telephone. The moss-hung woods surrounding the old shack that Mama Lovey and Papa had once owned were peopled by the strange eyes of owls. The woods were crowded by ancient trees that reached to the sky. The sky seemed to embrace their branches, which were so high up, Paige had to squint upward to see them. The air chimed with the drone of humming birds and whippoorwills. The bobolinks cried back and forth to one another. Cicadas vibrated providing a backdrop of music. Owls hooted sinisterly.

Paige was so afraid of the insect-wildlife infested air that she stayed inside. The only time she went out was when the adults went to town. During the day, she waited in the car with Uncle Lennie while Aunt Sunday and Aunt Mercy D went to the courthouse to see about the land. When Aunt Sunday didn't take Claudette inside with her, the two girls played hand pats. They had developed an elaborate system which Paige couldn't wait to get back and share with Smokey and Lee Esther.

"Claudette."

"Who's calling my name?"

"Claudette?"

"I'm playing a game."

"Claudette wanted on the telephone.

"If it ain't my baby, tell them I ain't home."

"Tick Tock. Listen to the tickin' on the clock Tick Tock."

On their last night in Shreveport, Aunt Sunday, Uncle Lennie, Wilmadine, Mercy D, and Claudette decided to go visit relatives. They left Paige with Wilmadine's five-year-old daughter, Grace. Deep in the woods, the sun only had a short debut before it was time to retire, so perhaps, it was only eight o'clock in the evening. In a child's mind, it was pitch black outside-bogeyman-ghost-ridden midnight. A

169

miasma of evil was palpable in the air. The wind blew through the boughs. The room, lit with candle light, cast flickering, dancing shadows on the walls. The owls howled insanely. In the oyster-lit moon, night hawks, buzzards, and bats swirled around the house.

"You know any ghost stories?" Grace asked.

"Yes," Paige replied, trying to sound brave. "You ever heard of Bloody Bones?" As Paige began to tell the story of Bloody Bones to her cousin, the floor boards creaked. The windows shook. The wind growled.

"Bloody Bones on the first step," Paige moaned. "Bloody Bones on the second step." Before Bloody Bones could make it to the third step, a noise pierced the room. Screaming and grabbing each other for cover, both girls almost fell off the bed. It was the phone ringing. Of all times, Luralee had decided to call that evening.

"Paige. Where is Sunday or Mercy D and them?"

"They're not here."

"What do you mean, they're not there? Who is there with you?"

"Grace."

"Who is that? Oh, Wilmadine's little girl!"

Whatever Luralee said after that was so incomprehensible to Paige, she didn't understand what was going on. She did understand the raging tone of her grandmother's voice, though. Upon their return to Tulsa, Paige witnessed the largest fight she'd ever seen grown folks—with the exception of her parents—have. Aunt Sunday stopped speaking to Paige from that point on. Even on the remainder of the train trip back home, she would not speak to Paige. She only spoke to Danny and Claudette. A black porter in a pristine white shirt was walking up the aisle of the train, when Paige noticed a large brown beetle on his back. The beetle was as large as the grasshoppers she'd seen in Tulsa.

"Oooh, look Aunt Sunday!" the child cried out.

"Shut up!" Aunt Sunday snapped. Those were the first and last words Sunday spoke to Paige before they returned to Detroit.

It had started out like any other sizzling, griddle-hot day in July. The lakes could be tasted on your tongue in every drop of moisture. Heat waves shimmered, shimmied and danced, forming skeleton mirages on the sidewalk. People were as irritable as a nest of scalded spiders.

Later, Jewel always said she'd had a sign. For one, she'd gotten off the bus, bone-tired and plain angry. While she was walking up Cottrow Street, she saw Solly, lolligagging with a group of his men friends, "looking like a monkey." The night before, she'd dreamed of a red room. This room represented a recurring dream Jewel had which went back to 1954, when Joe Boy, a jealous boyfriend, killed Millie, Miss Lenore's stepmother. The week that Millie had been slashed to death, Midge had awakened with a nightmare.

"Mama, I dreamed you had died," Midge sobbed. "I dreamed I was coming home from school, and they were bringing you out the house on a stretcher. Your arm fell out from under the cover and I just knew you were dead."

"Mama's going to be all right. I'll never leave you," Mama assured Midge. Unfortunately, when Millie had been killed just a few days after Midge's dream, it used to worry Jewel that perhaps there was something she could have done to have warned Millie. After the murder, people said that the walls were so splattered with Millie's blood, the room looked as if it had been painted red. At the funeral, the casket, much to the dismay of the gossipmongers, had to be closed, Millie had been so

172

mutilated. Nevertheless, Joe Boy had not served a day in jail for this crime. From that time on, whenever Jewel dreamed this dream, she became leery. They always said that Death traveled in threes.

On that particular blistering twilight when she got home, Jewel found out Danny, who was now almost fourteen, had been found drunk up at the neighborhood center. He'd sneaked out of the house to go to the canteen dance without permission. He was just the button Jewel needed pushed to send her rocketing into the ozone. Before she could give it a thought, she took Solly's leather belt from the door knob and gave Danny his last good whipping. Not much later, Solly came weaving in, half drunk. He was wearing Bermuda shorts, as if he might have been out to Belle Isle Park. This time when Jewel raised her voice in the war cry, Joey ran and handed Danny a meat cleaver and Paige a hammer. Out of nowhere, he pulled out a .22 gun and hit Solly over the head, because he was holding Jewel's flailing wrists.

"No, you're not, Nigger! That's my Mama."

Instantly, Solly sobered up. His eyes opened wide as a freshly-caught trout's eyes. He was in shock.

Finally, he found his voice. "I'm a kill you, little Nigger!"

Joey, who was never athletic, dashed with all the prowess of a natural-born sprinter out the back door. Half-drunk, Solly muttered out loud, "I'm leaving all y'all Niggers!" Because he had already wrecked several cars, Jewel hid his car keys under the mattress. But she hid his keys for more than that reason. She hid the keys, because frustrated as he made her, she still loved him. Finally, Solly climbed in bed and slept his "drunk" off. Joey slipped back into the house, later that evening.

If there ever was a death, it took place inside of Jewel.

That became the end of an era—"The Battle Royal," as she later dubbed the first twenty years of her marriage. After that day, Jewel and Solly never had another physical fight again. She'd already witnessed Judge leave home prematurely, after a wrestling-match-gone-awry with Solly. When Judge had joined the service at sixteen, lying on the sofa, playing the flutelike, soul-wrenching blues of "Nina Simone" and "Nancy Wilson," Jewel had almost drowned in her own soggy marsh of tears. The next year, when Cake Sandwich left and joined the air force, she began to get used to the idea of letting go of her "babies."

Because Joey had always been so quiet, Jewel had never realized how much animosity he had for Solly. "That Nigger told me he would send me to college, or any of us if we wanted to go. Now, here I want to go and he's talking about he doesn't have the money."

Joey complained on a daily basis to Jewel. She could only sigh. She didn't have any college money either. Why had Solly promised the boy? Joey was so vehement about his campaign for college, that one day Paige butted in and said, "Aw shut up!"

Joey reached over Jewel's shoulder and gave Paige a sock with his left fist in her right eye. Hearing the ruckus, Midge, who was already a mother and a wife, came downstairs from her room where she and her family rented, and jumped on Joey, fighting him the same way as when they were growing up. In the meantime, because Paige remained dark under her eye from that day forth, her classmates began to call Paige "Raccoon."

During that same week, Danny ran in two hours past curfew. It was almost eleven o'clock.

"Go get that belt, Nigger," Solly ordered.

"Daddy! Daddy! Listen. Listen. Lonny Rook just got killed. Ida Belle killed Lonny Rook." Within twenty-four hours, the story came out. Lonny Rook had been fighting Ida Belle for many years. They had seven children, Lee Esther, being one of them.

Whenever Ida Belle tried to report the violence she suffered at Lonny Rook's hands to the police, they refused to take action against him. For one thing, Lonny Rook was the biggest bootlegger and number runner Delray had ever seen. He made sure that all of the white police officers' pockets stayed lined with graft money, so there was never any hope of the law arresting Lonny Rook. In spite of his notorious deeds, he had been baptized Catholic so that all of his children could attend Catholic School. Quiet as it was kept, he even had a woman—he called her a distant relative—Olive, who lived under the same roof as his wife, Ida Belle. When Ida Belle went into labor with her last child, Cora Lee, a white police officer named Ray, had delivered the child in the ambulance. Although Ray became Cora Lee's godfather, when Lonny Rook broke Ida Belle's jaw, he didn't say a word, when she went to the police at Fort and Green station.

"If he hits me again, I'll kill him," Ida Belle reportedly told the police. The police hadn't believed her. Because of Ida Belle's promise, Danny Boy was spared a whipping from Solly's hands. Danny's friend's Ned's apartment window was directly across from the opened window where Lonny Rook's bullet-riddled body lay half-covered under a sheet, (in full view of the Delray spectators). Lonny had been taking his nap when Ida Belle emptied her shotgun in him. While the family sat around spellbound, Danny described in vivid detail how Lonny Rook's large stomach looked like a beached whale—only he had bullet holes in it and was dead. Ida Belle never served a day in jail, either.

As the children were growing older, Jewel found

herself swinging back and forth about her feelings about Solly. She would never forget the time they went to the concert at Belle Isle and he had carried a sleeping Paige, who by then, was at least seven years of age, with her legs dragging down to the ground. She also liked the way Solly walked five miles with her and the children to Patton Park and taught Paige and Danny how to swim the summer Paige was six.

Or, she'd never forget the time the entire family went to the drive-in to see the movie, "Imitation of Life," and Paige had been lost for more than half of the movie. Later, she found out the older children had seen Paige wandering up and down the dark graveled aisles, crying, yet refused to call her to the car. When the drive-in owner got on the loud speaker, announcing, "Will a member of the Shepherd family please come and get Paige Shepherd?"

Joey had finally gone to get her. The other children had said they were ashamed of Paige because she had twisted her hair in at least thirty little knots in the back of her head.

For the first time, Jewel was contemplating what she would do now that her children were getting older. She didn't want to finish raising any more children in Delray, but already Joey was graduating from high school. Joey had decided he would work and save up money to go to Highland Junior College. She had never seen a kid more determined than Joey. Whereas her older three children had a natural aptitude for school, none of them even considered college. They all had gone into the service or gotten jobs right out of high school. But Joey, her little below-average student, was the one with the grinding determination to tackle college. That was where Jewel's mind had meandered the day Paige came home with a crowd following her.

The Kilgores were a brawling bunch. Every weekend, in the middle of the night, sirens flashed, crowds gathered, curses split the air. Accompanied by the police's gruff, "Break it up! Break it up!", shattered glass interrupted a deep night's sleep. The two-story brick bungalow housed Granny Fay, her daughter, Liz, husband, Tootsie Roll, and a stream of transient men. Jewel never associated with this group. But Paige, who had grown up with Granny's granddaughter, Little Sister, frequented this haunt.

Little Sister, who was the smallest of Paige's group of friends, would fight down to her last ounce of snot-flying strength against anyone, no matter how often she lost. But she had a point to prove. "The bigger they come, the harder they fall." Her family's motto was, "If you can't beat a person, pick up a stick and hit them in the head with it."

That day as Paige walked home, carrying her violin, which she had been playing for four years, but was now contemplating quitting because it didn't look "cool" to play this "lame" instrument anymore, she popped the closed morning-glories growing on the fences along South Bend Street. Mauve, mother-of-pearl, and coral-pink lined the opened morning-glories. The bell-shaped heads quivered as bees swarmed about. Spring's green finger had waved a magic wand over the trees preening up South Bend. Watching the new buds open, Paige felt the first stirrings of adolescence blossoming inside her as she reveled in the heady fragrance of honey suckle. Cherry blossoms lit up the street like a lantern.

"You think you cute," she heard a voice from behind bait her. Paige turned around to see Little Sister.

"Go on, Little Sister. I done beat yo' ass enough. Now gon' 'bout your business." A few people ran off their porches. School children began to run up to signify.

"I wouldn't take that, Paige."

"Little Sister, you gon' let her talk to you like that?"

"Yeah, who says so?" Little Sister went on.

"I said so."

"I woulda won that last fight if you wasn't so tall. Knock this stick off my shoulder. Cross this line. I dare ya."

By the time the group had reached the corner of Cottrow, a fight was brewing. Grown-ups and school children alike gathered. Of all Jewel's children, Paige seemed to get into the most neighborhood fights. It was well known that she would fight not only her battles, but her friends' as well. But fighting was a fix to the Kilgores, not an exercise in defending yourself or standing up for the weak. Little Sister refused to let the fight go. She didn't like the jabot on Paige's blouse and could already see it in her hand, if she got a quick lick in. Paige saw Smokey and handed her the violin. By the time the two girls had fought up the street, Little Sister's lip was bleeding, although she had pulled the jabot off Paige's blouse and scratched her in the face. Little Sister went to get her infamous stick, but when she tried to swing it at Paige, Paige wrestled it out of her hand and hit her in the head with it. The crowd roared with excitement.

Suddenly, the people parted like the Red Sea, and Granny Fay, Little Sister's grandmother, came waddling up to Paige. Her intent was obvious. Before Granny Fay could bring her raised fist down at Paige, a quiet voice said, "Don't you dare hit my child."

The crowd became quiet and began to recede. Granny Fay froze, her arm still raised in midair. She looked at the smoldering beams in Jewel's eyes and weighed them. She had seen that look before in barroom brawls. It was the look of a lioness rising up to protect her cub. Moreover, it was the look that usually made the attacked person emerge victorious in a fight, leaving his challenger the worse off. Everyone waited, teetering on the cliff of excitement.

Silence reigned in the formerly boisterous street. People knew that Granny Fay was known to fight with grown men. No one ever heard of or knew about if Jewel ever fought with anyone.

Even Paige thought to herself, "Oh, Lord. Granny's Fay gonna kill Mama." Without a word, Granny Fay ambled, in her cowhand gait, back to her side of the street. The crowds dispersed.

It was years later Paige learned that Jewel had gone to jail only one time in her life. During World War II, while Solly was stationed at Fort Lewis, Washington, Jewel was working on a U.S. Navy ship in Richmond, California. Following an argument, she had taken a wire that she welded with and beat a white woman half-unconscious. The fight had been precipitated when the woman had continued to unplug Jewel's welding line, and called her "Nigger" when Jewel asked her to stop. They both went to jail and served time overnight.

That evening when Paige watched the news on television, a man named Martin Luther King, a new minister from the South, and a group of Negro followers, were being hosed and bit by dogs for trying to ride on the city bus and to eat freely in a restaurant.

"That wouldn't happen here," Paige thought.

A few months later, on the day before Thanksgiving, Paige came home from school to find Mama sitting before the television, eyes bleary with tears. "What's the matter, Mama?"

"President Kennedy's been assassinated."

"What's that?"

"He's been shot and killed."

Afterwards, the house became shrouded in a   funereal hush. Jewel didn't even make any dressing to go with the turkey she had baking in the oven.

With a bravado she didn't feel, Paige got up the nerve to bring up what was on her mind.

"Mama, I got something to tell you."

Jewel was so distraught that she didn't hear Paige.

Finally, Paige called her mother to the bathroom.

"What is it?"

"Come look."

When they went into the bathroom, Paige pulled down her panties and showed Jewel a patch of scarlet stain. Jewel felt a rush of mingled emotions. Her heart bifurcated into two rivers; one carrying feelings of grief for the slain president, and the other pumping floods of grief for her baby's lost girlhood. She had not taken into consideration that Paige was getting older. At forty-two, Jewel was already a   grandmother to three. The oldest three of her children had gotten married within months of each other and moved upstairs. She had her hands full, mediating and interfering in their affairs. Jewel remembered how stressed and frustrated she had been when Midge had begun her period. Because she didn't know how to handle it, she had been cruel. Passing down the only information she'd been handed, she'd snapped, "Keep you panties up and your dress down."

Trying to make up for her mixed feelings, tied up with her own first menstrual cycle which, in her memory, was a confusing ball of filth that went largely unattended, Jewel tried to remember what she would have liked to have been able to give to Midge, and what she wished someone had given to her. She ran a pan of lukewarm soapy water. With the gentleness of a mother bathing a newborn, she washed Paige up, gave her a belt and a sanitary napkin, then showed her how to put them on.

Afterwards, Jewel went outside to her favorite spot—her garden. She looked at her rosebush. Bereft of leaves, the rosebush looked like a naked, withered old lady. But Jewel still liked it. She had planted it the first spring she had moved to Delray. Now, she didn't mind when it turned fallow, because she knew, that unlike her annual flowers, it would re bloom. Although it would go underground like Persephone, the rosebush would return to the light of the sun when winter ended. In spite of her lack of pruning throughout the years, in spite of the winter storms, and even, in spite of, or perhaps because of, the children's tramplings, she knew her rosebush would array the back yard in all of its glory, come spring. The only living things that seemed to survive into the fall were the sunflowers lining her fence.

When Jewel was a child, Papa had taught her that the sunflower weeds were a curse to a garden. Jewel would have to pull these weeds out of the hard earth until her hands ached with calluses. But over the years, Jewel had noticed that the sunflowers that grew in Delray were like a blessing. They sent golden rays beaming through what was an otherwise barren yard. Better still, they drew rainbows of butterflies. She had even seen both gold finches and red robins hang upside down from the bean-like stalks, as they dug out the sunflower seeds in the open purple, maroon, and brown faces. Watching the sunflowers, the birds, and the butterflies had been like witnessing a little bit of heaven in her back yard.

A few days later, when they watched the funeral preparations on television, a thought bivouacked in Jewel's mind. A nation mourned the lost president. But who would mourn Lonny Rook besides his children? Ida Bell already had a new boyfriend. It made her think of Millie. Why hadn't the police arrested Joe Boy? Didn't a Negro woman's life matter? Or for that matter, didn't a Negro man's life count? Where would it all end? The same poison that assassinated the head was the same poison that had killed part of the body. How could anyone expect the body to be well, if the head was sick?

Suddenly, Paige interrupted her reverie.

"Mama. What are we going to do, now that the President's dead. My social studies teacher said that he was for colored people. That he was helping with the Civil Rights Movement."

Jewel was quiet and contemplative for a moment. A swinging door in her mind felt something close inside her. Just as the country was on the brink of a new beginning, she felt something ending, yet beginning anew inside her.

Finally, she answered Paige. "I guess we'll just have to go on and not give up."

THE PROMISED LAND

Epilogue 1993

"**A**re you sure there are no other reminiscences you'd like to share, Mother?"

Imani's voice leaned into the whirring sound of the video-camera recorder.

"Well, yes. I'd like to talk about our Caribbean cruises and our trip to Hawaii."

Jewel had once read a fairy tale where the Fairy Godmother had bestowed only one wish upon the Princess — to either have happiness when she was young, or to have happiness when she was old. Although young, the Princess was wise, and had chosen happiness when she was old, so that she would have something to look forward to in her golden years. Sometimes, Jewel felt that her life had kind of fallen in the same way. Taking everything into account, her older years had been all the happier for the trouble she'd seen as a young woman. Besides, she had a lot to be grateful for. She was close to all of her children, their children, and their children's children. She hadn't lived in Delray in over twenty-five years. And after her first set of children had grown up, with the luxury of raising only one child at a time, her lastborn — Imani — she had become very active in her new community and church. She was proud because all of her children were working. And if any one of them pointed out any "failings" — (Imani called it insanity, particularly since Cake Sandwich was prone to what the doctors called

The Ebony Tree

"nervousbreakdowns")—of the others, as Jewel once told Midge, "It's a miracle that the oldest three of you aren't all crazy." In fact, she'd gotten so close to Midge, whose adult life had been a foil to hers, that she had a new respect and admiration. Midge had divorced in her middle-twenties. Midge had been the free spirit, living her life, not answering to no one. Midge had not been the people pleaser....Sometimes she wondered, though. Had it all been worth it?

Taking the bitter with the sweet, even her sunset years with Solly had been idyllic, peaceful. After forty years of wandering in the wilderness of her life, she'd found happiness. What more could a woman, who started out her life more or less as an orphan, had asked for?

"Mom, I know about those. That was in the recent past. I want some family history."

Imani was getting impatient. She wondered how her mother, who had given birth to such a worldly traveler as herself, had lived such a boring life. Imani had a lifetime of memories of her mother waiting on her hand and foot, but she had no idea what the thoughts of this secretive stranger called "Mother" were. Without a doubt, she knew that Jewel had a smothering, hungry love for her. She constantly fought her mother's tendency to baby her. ("Get a life, Mother," was the theme of their battles.) Imani never realized that Jewel's children were her life.

At the same time, Imani knew she did not reciprocate Jewel's affection. After all, whoever said that the daughter would love the mother as much as the mother loved her? Wasn't that the way it was supposed to be? She could hardly wait to get back to the embassy in Moscow.

Looking on, trying to sort through the mother whom she had known, Paige smiled. She had finally lived long enough to appreciate how life's capricious foot could run combat boots through all of your false illusions.

Whenever Paige, then a rebellious teenager, tossed out some arrogant certitude, pointing out how "country" and "old-timey" she thought her mother was, Jewel used to say in a cryptic manner, "Just keep living."

Now, the only thing Paige knew for sure about anything was that as a mother, Jewel had been multifaceted, a diamond. With Paige, she had been a different person than the mother Midge had known... Or Imani had known. But, then again, how well does anyone ever know another human being?

Paige sighed. She had thought her life would be better than her mother's. At one time, she'd even thought that getting an education would be the passport. But with all the problems inherent in being a working, career mother, she felt her life, in an ironic way, had been worse than her mother's. Was it a case of the more things change, the more they stay the same? Well, maybe her life hadn't been worse, but surely more complex. It was a conundrum.

Over the years, Paige had often felt so trapped by all the demands as a working mother that she had wanted to run off. Had her mother ever felt that way? Was that what all the sighs used to be about? Why did women with small children sometimes feel enslaved? From her mother's lips, she'd never find out.

As far as Paige was concerned, the biggest issue for Black women of her mother's generation seemed to have been who, among the neighbors, had the whitest socks on their clothing line. Paradoxically, for all their degrees and independence, the Black women in Paige's generation seemed to deal with more loneliness. Among other perplexities, many of her friends were wondering why black men were seeming to prefer white women.

But the sad thing was that Paige couldn't even ask her mother what she had felt. How had she navigated through life's waters, yet still survived?

For sphinx-like, her mother's life would always remain a riddle to her children. Particularly to her daughters. Probably most of her secrets, Jewel would just take to the grave with her. Like the mother lode in a mine, good information would die untapped with her.

"We don't need to talk about it. It's too painful to talk about," would always be her unspoken motto.

Nevertheless, Jewel's life, like an underground cavern, replete with stalactite, stalagmites, and underground lakes, would always run in the hidden recesses of their blood. And on a windblown night, unrecounted memories of Oriole, Mama Lovey, and all the others, would haunt a sleepless dream.

No words. . . . No outcry. . ..No shame. . . .

When Imani ended the rolling tape, she asked, "Now are you sure you have nothing else to share other than how you went on Sunday School picnics with your kids?"

"No," Jewel said. "That's about all I remember." Through the lens, Jewel's eyes had filmed over. She was looking off into the distance, as if she could already taste the smoke rings of a Kool cigarette.

Order Form

Milligan Books
1425 West Manchester, Suite B,
Los Angeles, California 90047
(323) 750-3592

Mail Check or Money Order to:
Milligan Books

Name _____ Date _____

Address _____

City_____ State _____ Zip Code_____

Day telephone _____

Evening telephone_____

Book title _____

Number of books ordered ___ Total cost .... $_____

Sales Taxes (CA Add 8.25%) .... $_____

Shipping & Handling $3.00 per book .... $_____

Total Amount Due..$_____

· Check   · Money Order   Other Cards _____

· Visa   · Master Card   Expiration Date _____

Credit Card No. _____

Driver's License No. _____

Signature   Date